The King is Dead.

Stacy Riedel

Mrs Potts!
What am I
doing on tour??
I have no idea
either but I'm
sure loving the
ride. Thanks so much
for supporting me.
when's your
turn, woman??

BeeDubPub Independent Books

Milwaukee / Portland

All my
love,
Stacy Riedel

Published exclusively by BeeDubPub Independent Books

Milwaukee, WI/Portland, OR

www.thekingisdead.com

First Paperback Edition

Keep away from open flame, bodies of water, and coffee cups, as this first edition may be worth a hefty sum one day.

Library of Congress Cataloging-in-Publication Data

Riedel, Stacy

      The King is Dead. / by Stacy Riedel – 1st ed.

         p. cm.

      ISBN 978-0-615-37638-7

Designed by Stacy Riedel, Kati L. Dowling

Printed in the United States of America

Acknowledgements

I would like to thank the countless friends and family that supported this endeavor. You know who you are, because I've bothered to call you on your birthday when most of the time I'm not even sure what the date is. I'm forever changed by you and hope to serve you well.

I share this with you and wish to extend special gratitude to a particular few:

Kati L. Dowling, for bringing me back to this business by brute force, and for her tireless editing and objective eye.

Zach and Cash Saucier, my generous cover models who saved my ass at the midnight hour.

Christine Chevalier, who brought it to my attention nearly twenty years ago that there was a career out there for me.

Hank and Pat Riedel, because every kid should be raised by people who are willing to take risks and explore their infinite possibilities.

Erin Potts, because she reminded me impatience is good, that we get old, we get sick, and we run out of time, so let's get living already.

"Out beyond ideas of
wrongdoing and rightdoing,
there is a field.
I will meet you there."
–Jalal ad-Din

· The King is Dead

"Ma'am would you like us to perform an autopsy?" the gentleman in the scrubs asked her delicately. He muted his voice, like an audible expression of his bland blue scrubs, the most inoffensive color in the spectrum behind *sand*. Like his entire being was the very definition of unobtrusiveness, as though showing up to work one day and delivering such bad news in red scrubs would be like tap dancing on a grave. Lorraine thought at this moment he appeared more stricken than her, and she found it all very comical. His meandering, monotone way of speaking coupled with arched brows and stressed frown lines, she thought he was presently operating on slo-mo. Had she taken a barbiturate and forgotten about it?

"Why? Do you think you might be able to bring him back to life?"

"Sometimes, in these situations, it brings some comfort to know why people pass."

Lorraine thought this was ludicrous. "People waste too much time on 'why,' Doctor. People die." What does Why change? People who find out the Why spend the rest of their lives warning other people about the dangers of red meat, sun exposure, sedentary lifestyles. To her, it was obnoxious. Lorraine preferred smoking, staying up late, and never, ever asking why.

This poor doctor in his baby bland scrubs feared her in this moment, which he should have. Sure, she was an old lady, clearly alone in this emergency room holding area, looking frailer than when she came in. But he was used to more vulnerability at this point in the process. Something about her posture and the angle of her chin relative to the floor, perfectly parallel, made him believe she was the smartest person in the room, and could use her power for evil. "I understand," he was 32, he didn't understand, "I just want you to know we did everything we could."

"Of course you did," which coming from Lorraine was an insult. *Of course you did, you fetus.*

"Do you have some family you can call?"

She was reluctant to answer. Yes and no. Mostly no.

"Would you like us to call someone for you?"

"Why would I want that?" Lorraine squeezed her hands together, and the doctor could see the translucence of her skin was between them, little blue veins coursing through them like a map back to the safety of her beating heart. "Were you under the impression I'm unable to dial a telephone?"

"No, but-"

"As you can clearly see, I have fingers. Oh, dear are you blind?" she condescended.

"No, my apologies," the doctor sputtered like an old car, jarred by her directness. He couldn't function in the presence of such control. "I just thought it might be easier for you to sit and let us do that for you." He was beginning to realize she wasn't one of those panicked old widows suddenly left with the world to herself. The self-sufficient ones were the worst kind.

"In that case I'd love a ham sandwich. And is there someone who could come and file my corns down? That would be easier than me doing it."

"I just-"

"I just!" Lorraine cut him off. "I just, I just. Never Just something, Doctor. Do it or don't, but never apologize."

From there it was a staring contest. She waited for him to relent, because people always relented to her, because she made the decision long ago as a girl never to be the first to blink.

There was paperwork to sign, which Lorraine was thankful a charge nurse with some attitude and a name with no vowels provided for her, instead of this baby for a doctor they'd put to the task of saving lives and empathizing with people he couldn't possibly empathize for. The nurse was happy not to have to mop up more tears that day, and efficiently this partnership generated all the necessary signatures, and more quickly than usual, Lorraine was out on the sidewalk. She stared at her little car out there in the lot, seemingly segregated from the other, less tragic cars. A street lamp shone down on it like a beacon. *Welcome to the rest of your life*, it said to her.

Out in the car she was thankful for the solitude. No more prying eyes in the waiting room, no EMS workers questioning her ability to fend for herself, however subtly so, no doctors reminding her to eat, as though one could ever forget. What a garish spectacle an emergency room can be.

She asked herself what the next step was. Call the kids? The funeral home? A lawyer? None of that sounded right. "Pie," she said aloud to herself, and cranked the ignition forward.

The yellow car ran like a dream even to this day, although now it appeared she'd be having a stranger maintain it instead of Frank. She'd grown so used to the luxury of Frank's handy work, likening taking her car to a mechanic to meeting her new gynecologist. There was such a strange intimacy to it that moving on to a paid mechanic felt like adultery.

The car hummed and Lorraine's eyes wandered to the little sticker on her windshield. It read that she had another thousand miles before she'd need an oil change. She fast forwarded her brain to that point in time and wondered in what state Frank would be. Would he have skin? How much do people decompose in the ground, in a box? When does a body go from being remains to a corpse, to fertilizer? What's the timeline on this one? She'd be waiting on her car at the lube place and he'd be gooey.

And why the burial? Frank was about as religious as a coin toss. It never occurred to her to buy a plot, but Frank had that little detail squared away years ago. Worse, he hadn't even bothered to secure her a spot nearby. When she confronted him, back when he wasn't a dead guy, he only said, "I shouldn't have to do all the thinking for you," because he'd slowly retreated from that over their life together. In the early years he wouldn't pass a bakery without picking up a fresh donut for her, but toward the end he bypassed that road on purpose, avoided the little courtesies, stopped checking to see that she'd remembered to flick off the power on her space heater. "Why didn't you remind me? We could have burned the house down!" But

Frank just spit out his robotic response like an ATM chit, "I shouldn't have to do all the thinking for you."

The plot though, that one got her goat. She could handle an old man growing too tired to pick up a pastry, but to proactively seek out an eternal resting place, secretly, to do the leg work and ask the questions and sign the contracts, all without her input or inclusion, well, the implications were insulting. "What are you going to do with me if I die first?" she asked him.

"Trust me, woman, that ain't going to happen."

"Well, what if it does?"

"That isn't really my responsibility, now is it? I took care of my business, now you take care of yours." Lorraine couldn't decipher if this was his typical insensitive pragmatism, the equivalent of him asking for cash as a birthday present, maybe one final escape attempt *from beyond*, or if in his mind this was the gracious thing to do, to take the burial decisions out of her hands during her time of grieving. At this point it didn't matter the Whys. The fact remained that here she sat alone, with nowhere to rot and no one to do it with.

In the car she made the decision to be a fraction of a percentage grateful that most of her work was done here. She need only make a phone call or two, show up in something funeraly, and voila, body in the ground. "Bing, bang, boom," as Frank used to say. Much easier than speculating on her husband's intentions.

Lorraine cranked up the volume on the stereo. There was no tape deck, certainly no CD player, "The right song comes to you, not you to it," Frank always reminded her, but still she fiddled the dial for the right station. There it was, near the top of the AM channels, Elvis Presley. Frank reminded her of Elvis when they first met. Blue collar jaw line, sideburns that couldn't have been carved any cleaner, and a singing voice deep enough she could feel it under her feet, like a charging steam train.

She put the car in reverse and sought out some pie. The pedal met the floor and Lorraine was weaving through the streets of greater Milwaukee at Audubon speed, feeling no more limitations in her life, not time, space, or miles per hour. The car kicked up leaves in every direction, and she rolled down the window just a hair to get a hint of that almost-winter smell in her face. "You still got it, baby," she cooed to Elvis, feeling a lonely sort of freedom wash over her.

"Love Me Tender" percolated through her ears like Frank was right next to her. The next thing she knew she was at a 24-hour truck stop diner and had no memory of driving there. Like her entire life, a turbo charged expedition with no idea how so much had happened before she could react. She'd learned years ago to stop asking for a time machine, accepted there were no do-overs, no such thing as a clean slate. But in this crisp night she would have given everything to rewind it all, take herself to the song, instead of the song to her.

Whiplash

Tim got on the road around six that day, a little earlier than he would normally be awake, which surprised his roommates. They were used to his usual routine of snoring, ass scratching, and indifference until at least 11 in the morning. Usually he eased back to life gradually, sluggishly and complaining the whole way, making gravelly noises and leaving phlegm piles in the sink the way smokers generally do in the morning. Strangely this particular dawn he was clear and alert, and his roommates wondered if the clunking around he made gearing up for the trip was a dream or that sub-state of waking life where a little bit of the real world mixes with the sleep world, and an alarm clock chime works its way into subconsciousness as an ambulance siren, and the dreamer snaps awake to believing they're being hustled to a hospital. Tim's preparations this morning included filling the cooler with snacks and energy drinks, moving his duffel bag from here to there, running the shower. The commotion sounded to his dreaming roommates like what it would sound to be squished in a trash compactor, like snow shoes shuffling through the woods, like swimming at the edge of Victoria Falls. If only a road trip back to the Midwest was just that exciting.

In fact coming home to the funeral of a man who never loved him wouldn't seem like a priority in any other case. He'd only been given a day's notice, just another testament to how inconsiderate that man had always been.

An inexplicable fire charged him up and out the door and onto those wet roads.

Tim hadn't made the trip in ten years, and even that was going in the opposite direction. But the heart never forgets great journeys. His first great journey was getting the fuck out of Dodge. Turning around and going back after all this time, he was afraid of getting there and being stuck, a castaway in the state of Wisconsin, swallowed by a state the rest of the country forgot about if it wasn't football Sunday. His last girlfriend asked him, aloud and with her own mouth, if Wisconsin was somewhere in Nova Scotia. He told her it was.

Leaving Portland Tim saw in his rearview the dew soaked bridges that once signaled the end of his old life. Those bridges were a comfort to him, and now he was leaving their loving arches to return back to his sisters, who had begged for a reunion since he was 16, not even seven days after he'd fled. They called him "the baby," still did. Now he was 26 and those ten years getting by, some of the longest in anybody's life, suddenly felt like a flash of occasional shoplifting, acoustic strumming in the bus depot, the random yard sale furniture find, feeling like just one long month, happening too fast, like whiplash.

Driving into the sunrise, enough quiet passed over him to think to his inevitable: whether he was destined for struggle, and if so, could he ever enjoy a life meant to drag him down at every triumph. He'd asked himself the grave questions, wondering when anything got easy, and had never come up with a glorious answer. Leaving home so young was supposed to be his liberation, a good story one day, his badge of honor among the hooligans he ran with those first few years. But all that followed was a plague of uphill battles and short-stay jail sentences: weed possession, drunk driving, resisting arrest, squatting, and any other general disorderly conduct that screamed "childhood demons."

The slow rise from that pit didn't inspire a ton of hope, if he was really honest with himself. For the time being he was at least employed, even if it was somewhere he didn't want to admit aloud to anyone but the lowlifes in his band, certainly not to a girl. And he had roommates, which meant he had an apartment, which meant he typically had something to eat, and somewhere to warm his rain soaked feet every night. So how come it didn't *seem* easier? When would it? Was any of this worth the goddamn trouble? His mind went there in his solitude.

Despite previous depths of self loathing, considering whether he wanted to wake up the next day at all, he still drove on back home and not off a cliff.

A Facelift

A sexy BMW with blacked out windows slithered up along the "Arrivals Pick-Up" and came to a stop, awaiting the blonde who soon enough appeared from baggage claim. A steady fog wafted out the tail pipe, and every so often the mysterious driver would rev his engine as a reminder he was there. Prominent lips and a round, overexposed décolleté, despite temperatures dipping into the 30s that day, the girl emerged from the automatic doors like a mirage, as though floating along the heat waves radiating off desert sand. Milwaukee isn't known for its tropical weather, yet here she glided along like her cleavage knew no bounds. It must breathe free. The mom-jeans wives and little league coach husbands from her flight all stared conspicuously as she oozed into the passenger seat and was whisked away. Women privately fumed, men swallowed. That fantasy passed.

But wait! I'm here, too, Aubergine's subconscious yearned at all these strangers. For some reason when the blonde passed through them, the automatic doors zipped open effortlessly, but for Aubergine they clunked along their tracks as though irritated by the disturbance. She stepped out into the cold and stared at her breath. It had been a while.

Despite dragging behind her a Louis Vuitton roller, the Gucci sunglasses, the tell-tale red soles of her Louboutin heeled boots, no one cast a glare her way. She fully expected to stand out in this crowd, she had since the day she was born, but here she was amidst the Jordache crowd, and no one could be bothered to wonder who she was. This was a frustration she'd come to find all too familiar as the years dragged across her face and career like a pick-up on a gravel road.

Suddenly her sister's greige Astro Van pulled up like a lump and a familiar face waved and wiggled from the driver's side window. Aubergine's heels cleared the ground by a couple inches as she bounced like a little girl. "Sissy!" The van screeched to a clumsy stop and shoved into park, and Aubergine's sister bounded out of it unaware of the lane of traffic whizzing by her without regard.

"Auby!" Screams, squeals, incomprehensible chirps, hugs, one sister cupping the other sister's face, then the reverse, tears, and like a dust devil they were off.

"Aubergine Gladney, would you look at yourself?" Bluebell buzzed at her sister, trying to drive and take in everything that had changed since their last meeting. "Every time I see you, you're a little more Hollywood."

Compliment? "Do I? Everyone in L.A. says I look so Midwestern it's painful." Her first agent, during a final dust-up, said she was about as polished as a Lake Winnebago walleye.

"Auby, you are home! You are *home!*"

Aubergine attempted shared glee, figured it would be better to go along with this little charade than point out that like her brother, she got out, and she got out fast, and she tried every day to shake off Milwaukee like a wet dog. "Shh, shh, hang on. If I don't concentrate on this road I'm never going to figure out how to get back on the freeway. You'd think I'd never been to the airport before."

Auby obliged her and took the moment to examine Bluebell's latest look. Short, round haircut sprayed to a soft yet immobile meringue, green turtleneck with a yellow Green Bay Packers logo on it, khaki pleated pants, humble wedding ring and pearl stud earrings. *Jesus, Sissy, you're only 37.* Of course a Wisconsin 37 is a California 52.

"So how's showbiz? I haven't seen you in the papers in a while, thank GAWD. They had you paired with so many bozos I finally just stopped believing it all."

Aubergine hated that her sister, the one who was supposed to rise above this tabloid nonsense, ever gave those rags any credence in the first place. "You're telling me you did at one time believe that stuff? I told you it was all bullshit they make up to sell magazines."

Bluebell responded quickly, always the energetic and eager of the Gladney girls. "Oh, of course not! I thought to myself, Auby would never date a rodeo clown."

"He was a bull rider."

Bluebell was not relieved by this fun fact. "Aubergine, you dated a bull rider? How does one even meet a bull rider?"

"How does anyone meet anyone? Your paths cross, you fall in love, next thing you know there are cameras following you to the bathroom. It's not a big deal. It's L.A. I don't know what to tell you."

Bluebell lurched, "No need to get so defensive, Sissy, I was just asking."

"Well, I'm five minutes off the plane and already getting a lot of flack here. Do you see me asking how you met Mark? Who gives a shit?"

"Aubergine Gladney," Bluebell pointed sternly to the crucifix hanging from the rearview mirror.

"Oh, Jesus Christ."

"And for your information, the reason you don't have to ask where I met my husband is because you know my answer doesn't involve cameras following us to the toilet. God brought us together. In church!"

"Quit yelling at me!" Just like old times, Aubergine fumed. It didn't take five minutes. Like that mysterious sports car back at the airport, zero to sixty in a whoosh.

The van swerved, Bluebell was a bit worked up. "And don't act like you're suffering," miming a violin being played, no hands on the wheel, "just because you can't have a sex affair with a rodeo clown in a public restroom without the papparonis catching it all on film. You chose that life, Auby." To be fair, she did.

Aubergine threw her hands up and let out a phluff of frustration. "I don't even know what to address with that. Let's start with how you got to this day and age in the same America I live in, and yet you can't seem to pronounce the word 'paparazzi.'"

Bluebell, stunned, looked at her sister blankly, unsure of why of all points she could have made, some valid, Aubergine corrected her pop culture vocabulary. The van was quiet a good, pregnant minute.

"You should get over, or else you're going to miss our exit," Aubergine offered, considerably calmer, the red from her face receding back to a pinkish sort of flush.

"Thank you," Bluebell responded, flicking on her blinker. A thick pause hung in the air like they were speeding down the freeway in a car full of pudding. This is what they did, every time. Go nuts during the initial reunion, spend a few minutes quietly judging each other, then the yelling, then the awkward tension of too much truth. Bluebell was just glad to have an ally back to town. In her home she was a wife and a mother and defined by those things, and Aubergine, her baby sister, was a breath of fresh air. "It's good to have you back, Sissy."

Aubergine reached out to Bluebell and they held hands the rest of the drive. The roads rocked the van, as Milwaukee roads are so untamed they could have been imported from Kabul. Auby had forgotten about that little detail, since Los Angeles roads certainly possess their own unpredictability, but by and large they're smooth. "These roads could sure use a face lift," everything was an aesthetic reference to her. She held her new breasts as her sister maneuvered the van over the bumps, weaving to avoid potholes.

"Milwaukee has always needed some work. Only the strong survive here."

"That's why I left," Aubergine responded curtly. But Bluebell knew there was nothing weak about her sister. "No it isn't," she bit back, letting go of Aubergine's hand to turn the wheel a sharp left.

Snap

The last conversation between Frank and Lorraine wasn't so much a conversation as it was a referendum.

They'd been together 38 years, not long compared to their friends' marriages, even though to them 38 years was the oldest they ever planned on living in the first place. They would have rather spent their 38th year in the papers due to a failed parachute opening or a tumble down Kilimanjaro or a rollercoaster malfunction. BUNGEE CORD SNAPS FOR AGING THRILL SEEKERS would be the headline. It would be fairer to say Frank made it well beyond their 38th year and died of boredom instead.

He'd had some beers. Lately Frank had always had some beers. They were in the kitchen and Lorraine was snapping stems off green beans for about the thousandth time in their life together, and Frank was watching. "That's a nice blouse you got on, Lorrainey." She did love this particular color on herself. Magenta with swirls of beads in every shade of red and pink in large crop circle style patterns down the front and the back. Wearing it always brought her a burst of energy and she smiled at her reflection every time. "How much did it set me back?"

"Well, I bought this in 1983," she stopped snapping to look at her sweater and calculate its value, "so would you like the original price, or should I adjust for inflation?" She challenged him with her eyes. The latter half of their marriage had been one big cock fight.

He waited for the point to pass, and she continued on preparing his meal. "How come you always sound like you're from Paris or somethin'?" Indeed she did have a bit of a cosmopolitan flair that stood out like royalty in Milwaukee. She always believed she was born 1500 miles too far west.

"Why do you always insist on being a plebian?"

"I do not," his old man jowl quivered at the accusation.

"That you even know what a plebian is means you aren't one. So give up the act. There are Gs at the end of some of your words. Somethin'. Nothin'. You're no cowboy." *Snap... snap... snap...* just the sound of her work. It had been longer than she could remember since the last time he snapped his own beans.

"Don't forget to salt those before you put those in the oven."

"I think I know how to make beans, Frank. If you lost the weight I've put on you over the years, it would be like birthing a calf. It's safe to say you trust my cooking."

"Don't get so defensive. You just forgot the salt once. I didn't want you fucking up my meal again. It's my one pleasure in life."

Lorraine lifted the colander from the sink, shook down the drain whatever water had collected between the beans, then slammed the whole thing onto the linoleum floor. Steam, beans, and general ruckus scattered all over the place, including Frank's boots that sat nearby awaiting something to crawl down in them. The colander bounced this way and that, balancing on its rim until settling upside down in one final sputter.

Frank didn't move, unsurprised. He was no stranger to his wife's fits, however sudden. Lorraine smoothed her blouse and looked soberly down her nose at him. Calmly, she raised a finger to him, "I forgot the salt twenty-six years ago, Frank Gladney. And if your only pleasure in life is food, my food, perhaps you should learn how to talk to your cook. Because I can forget the salt every day for the rest of your goddamn life if I want to."

Frank stood from his seat and put his hands on his hips. Sometimes he stood just to prove how much bigger than her he was, like an old silverback gorilla.

She wouldn't admit it, but she trembled inside. Lorraine was that other type of victim that never succumbed completely, taking all the pleasure out of it for Frank. The abuse went both ways, if she had anything to say about it.

Frank knew better, decided to leave it. He fetched his boots from the other end of the kitchen, shook them loose of their bean shrapnel, and was gone out the back door. She had one last retort in her, she always had one last retort, but the door slammed shut and her shoulders jumped.

Lorraine inhaled deeply to calm herself. She leaned against the sink and watched him walk down the road without a coat, going nowhere in particular, kicking up all sorts of dust along the way. She wondered how many of these outbursts of his were legitimate expressions of his discontent, and how many were self-tests of whether he had the resolve to walk out the door and disappear already, for good this time. One day he'd vote with his feet, she knew. And it was always in the very second following a bean throwing fit that she realized this sort of behavior was exactly what he needed to push him over the edge. Exhibit A for the prosecution: Beans in shoes.

Chains

Around Nebraska Tim started to sweat. The nearness of his hometown was apparent with every passing cornfield, every dusty pick-up. He'd been on the road over a day, he knew that for sure, having seen one full sunset and two sunrises, all on one thirty minute roadside nap. One could mistake this rush to get home with eagerness to be there instead of eagerness to get the whole rigmarole over with.

Once again the gas light blinked on and Tim pulled off the road to one of those little fill-up stations you only see in middle America. Two pumps with no concept of credit card functionality, perfectly comfortable with pump *then* pay, the owners never bothering to even lay down some asphalt. His gray Festiva jumped and bumped over the uneven drive, finally settling to be refueled.

Tim's boots and pants thunked and clinked along the dirt as he made his way up to the attendant. He may as well have been wearing spurs with all the jingle-jangly accoutrements hanging off his body. "Fill up on..." he looked back to where he was parked, trying to determine a pump number.

"You're the only car out there, son. I can figure it out." The man behind the counter smiled, swiped Tim's card, trying not to stare. "It'll be just a minute." Tim waited. The man's face was extremely tan and whiskery. Tim was pale and could never grow a beard to save his life. "Warm one out there." Tim sighed. *A minute in Nebraska is like…* "Think we're supposed to get to 45." …*water torture*. This might have been the longest credit card transaction ever, according to Tim's patience. The old man leaned up against the counter, used to this process. "You in some sort of… *rock band*?" he asked, emphasizing rock band as though speaking another language. Tim nodded, "I could tell. On account of the chains." Indeed, the figure eight of chains looping from one hip to the other and back again was a complicated outfit to get into. "It'll be just a minute."

Tim waited, tapping his fingers on the counter in a complicated percussion that only made him more anxious, drumming long enough to consider what a life like this was. Would he feel better or worse living in this nondescript world where he could actually be anonymous? Moving to Portland so long ago was an attempt to leave identity behind, but he'd certainly carved out a pigeon hole for himself, adopting a sort of persona that felt comfortable at the outset. Maybe putting on some coveralls and moving out to the sticks to have two minute relationships with strangers was truer to his life's mission of disappearing completely. Wearing eyeliner did him no favors outside of his band life.

The credit card finally received its signal from the moon and spit out a receipt for him to sign. "Thanks," he mumbled.

"Yep," the old man carried on, as though this much leather walks through the door every day. "Where you headed?"

"Uhhh. Home. I guess. Milwaukee." Nothing about that sentence felt natural.

The old man found this amusing. "Beer and cheese."

Tim was more than used to this reaction. No one he'd ever met had anything else to say when he reported he was from Milwaukee. "Don't forget the Packers."

The attendant popped the chit into a small unlocked box that sat on top of the counter unguarded most of the day. "That's right. The state church of Wisconsin." Tim was impressed. A hint of irreverence coming from a man located in the center of obscurity. Where he developed a sense of humor out there in those corn fields was anybody's guess.

Tim smiled, "Praise be," and was on his way. The old man put two fingers to his forehead and saluted lazily. For people living on the coasts, it's easy to forget these people exist all together.

The Bundles

Tim scanned his MapQuest printout one last time to make sure he was pulling up to the right house. He shook his head at the likeliness of it all. Ivy on the clapboards. Geometric patterns mowed into the lawn. White wrap-around porch. "Fuckin' A, Bluebell. A minivan?" he asked his sister out of her earshot.

"Timmy!" his sisters hollered in unison, running from the front door to his car in a blue streak. Small children ran around in a zigzag making it impossible for him to count them all. He wondered if he was just tired and hallucinating, or if his sister was operating an illegal child mill.

Bluebell's husband waited at the door for the siblings to get past the initial hugs and tears. Tim waved hello but was too overrun by sisters to notice if Mark signaled back. "Hey, Sissy," Tim repeated to the girls, embracing them long enough to convince them it felt good. "Christ, Auby, you got skinny." She was going for a "meat in all the right places" kind of look, by any means necessary. He tried to hug her through her new boobs, but couldn't quite get the feel of her besides those bony arms. He was disappointed, but didn't say so.

"That's what I told her. We're going to have to feed her while she's home. No more of those milkshakes made out of grass and raw fish." Auby and Tim exchanged a puzzled furrow, wondering which gossip rag she'd pulled that from. "And you, too, Mister." Bluebell, always the mom. She slung an arm around his neck and spoke closely to him, "Do me a favor and don't take the Lord's name in vain while you're here, okay?"

"Yeah, sorry," he answered flippantly. "Going to take me a day or two to get back in the groove."

"I know, baby brother. I'm just so happy you're here! Bad circumstances, but shoot, a reunion is like a party where everybody is the guest of honor. Now come on over here and meet my little ones." The rascals giggled and screamed as they ran around in circles for no discernable reason.

Auby had one over her shoulder, squeezing in all the spots that generated a belly laugh. "Let's go meet Uncle Timmy," she said, corralling them as best she could.

All four of them stood in a sort of queue before him, bundled up in countless layers, their breath crystallizing from the holes in their hooded jackets. He couldn't make out their faces behind their steam. "This one here is Wilson, that's Wendy, Watson, and William."

"Christ, how can you tell?" All four were so padded with garb, all about the same height, one couldn't tell if they were male, female, or someone else's kids all together.

"Language!" one of them yelled, he had no idea which.

Aubergine chimed in, "Sissy, I just realized you named one child Wilson, and the other William. Isn't that a little confusing?"

"Why is that confusing? They're two completely different names."

"Are they?" Tim asked.

"What are you talking about?" getting defensive now. "William, Wilson, William, Wilson. Not even close."

Pause.

"Don't teachers get confused?" Aubergine asked.

"They're four."

Tim felt his genitals clench and his skin blow back as though he'd walked into a wind tunnel. "All of them?!"

Mark waved them all inside, welcoming Tim in particular with a giant bear hug and an odd choice of a kiss on the cheek. They hadn't seen each other since the wedding when he was just a teenager. Apparently Mark really missed him. *Really* missed him. "Beware all ye who enter here!" he bellowed in his theatrical baritone. Tim just then remembered his brother-in-law's knack for well placed references.

Tim and Aubergine shared a shiver and crossed the threshold.

Capo

When Lorraine set her sights on Frank he was exactly her type. Diplomatically speaking, he had swings of exuberance, depending on the moment. For whatever reason, boorish behavior is sexy to a young girl, even if it is embarrassing to a woman. A woman wants a man who brings her pretty things in pretty little boxes. But a girl just wants the boxer.

Frank was home on leave, was "looking for some pussy," and he said so. His friends from high school all laughed at his vulgarity and appreciated that though they'd all gone different routes- two to the Navy, one to college, one to Canada, one to the Army- Frank never lost that charm.

"Look at all these beautiful girls," he said to whomever in the bar was closest, he didn't care who heard. All of them looked hungry, their hair pinned perfectly and sprayed to a wig-like appeal, their sweaters snug enough to show ribs underneath, their pencil skirts so tight that a pencil couldn't fit beyond the waistband, the slits up the back modified to reveal just a little more thigh. A slight bend over the jukebox and a keen eye could catch a hint of girdle, which of course was every girl's intention. Frank saw right through them, these easy targets.

One girl stood out among the others, the story always goes, and that of course was Lorraine. In a dank, smoky bar the crowd seemed to part, like a literal path right to his future. She cast her lure without even trying.

He looked at her and thought about how much he would probably hate her. She was the only girl in the place with long and unruly hair, some of it curly, some just a little wavy, like all she'd done was flip her head over, shake it up real good and leave the house. She had no bra, a guy his age could spot that a mile away. Her nipples were sharp against her dress, which at the time did not follow the trend. His friends caught him staring. "Seeing more and more of those at school," the college kid said.

All the other girls followed the rules, cinched and poofed and looking for husbands. This girl didn't scan the room like the others. She stood in her space in a relaxed posture, one hand on her hip, the other twirling the hem of her dress in knots around her finger.

"I'm not sure how I feel about it." He bit a fingernail absently. "Women should be women." Frank was much more comfortable with traditional gender roles. Men were men, and women were constricted.

"I don't know man, those are the ones you want. If all you're looking for is pussy, I mean."

College kid was right. The sweater girls were thinking long term, or at least that was the image they were trying to project, so that even if they did just want someone for the night, they assumed faux purity was the only way to it. Either way it was an expensive and tiring little game, being the polite guy paying for drinks all night, gambling on whether or not this was a girl interested in going all the way, but not all the way to the altar. Not that far.

But Nipples across the room, the one all the other girls were utterly disgusted by, she appeared a little less motivated, certainly breathing a little easier.

Abruptly the bar owner cut the record that was playing and welcomed Lorraine to the stage. Frank sat a little taller in his booth to see as much as he could without making too much effort, or appearing to anyway, but eventually the crowd of people blocked his view anyway. "Please give a warm round of applause to Lorraine Saves the Dave!" A tepid reception, and then Dave began.

"One, two, one two three four," he could be heard saying just off the mic, and his acoustic started in.

Lorraine tapped her tambourine softly, "There somethin' happenin' here," her voice was husky and sweet, a little too sweet for the song's heavy message. "What it is ain't exactly clear…"

Dave came in on the harmony, "There's a man with a gun over there they-uh…" Not Frank's favorite song, but was sung beautifully, even to a guy who mostly avoided beautiful things.

The college kid had a view of the stage, the only one of his group. "That girl is… Wow. She's very different." Frank saw his friend gulp down his hormones.

"If you're into that peace shit," Frank said, glugging back his beer.

"I'm into whatever she's into," College Kid said, adjusting the glasses on his face nervously. The attraction might have been purely physical, she was creamy and soft and glowed among the spackled tigresses. More likely it was because she was the closest to a sure thing in the bar, what with her progressive beliefs and detachment from social mores. Whatever it was, Frank felt a twinge of competition stirring in him.

Before the song could end, the small crowd before the stage began to turn on Lorraine Saves the Dave. A few people swayed with their eyes closed, but otherwise this was a pretty hawkish youth, and the song worried their commie-fearing hearts. A woman wearing a pearly brooch booed, feeding the fury. Dave kept strumming, but Lorraine was clearly off balance. Her voice rasped a little harder, her eyes zeroing in on individual hecklers, like a bull readying to charge.

"Keep going, Dave," she said into the mic, looking a little purposed. Frank listened with a smirk on his face. Lorraine lectured the crowd. "The proletariat will always be happy with their strings pulled," she mimed an evil puppeteer, College Kid guffawed in amazement, "independent thought is a threat, it's always safest to put your hands in the lives of strangers, of the epaulets in Washington, sending our brothers off to die," Dave played harder, his head down and swinging athletically to the beat, more passionately now, "these men lay down their lives, and for what? Why are they fighting again?" The boos grew and molded into a rolling thunder.

"Holy shit! Someone threw a shoe at her!" College Kid reported. "I don't think this is going to hold." Breaking glass could be heard on stage. "This is going to get ugly," his eyes widened, amused.

Frank and his buddies suddenly felt the urge to witness whatever bloodbath was brewing and rushed from their booth to the back of the crowd.

Lorraine noticed Frank in uniform just beyond the stage light and smiled. *How topically cute*, she thought to herself. She could barely make out a face. It was the expression that caught her attention. A bottle whizzed by Dave's head, jostling him enough to give up and try again another night. Wrong crowd, he surmised. "Get outta here, ya bums!" someone yelled as they ducked objects and scooted off stage. The proletariats cheered victoriously, thinking with enough bullying the peace movement would go away. It was growing enough in numbers and newspapers to start to rile the straights.

"Damn, these people sure hate peace," College Kid found the whole scene astonishing. The crowd chased her out like an old stray cat. Dave had to leave his guitar case behind and open on stage, vulnerable to angry bladders, just to get away safely. "Think she's out back?" The bar emptied into an alley, where beer and liquor trucks unloaded their deliveries twice a week, and where the seedier elements seemed to find comfort. "I bet she parties."

Frank, in uniform, declined. "I don't think she's interested."

"Maybe not in *you*," College Kid quipped. "See ya, chumps!" and begged off. He disappeared into the mass of celebratory Republicans and out the back door.

The night wore on and Frank sobered up. The girls bored him, even the ones pretending to be bad, and so he called it a night. Tucking his hat under his arm and throwing a five spot on the swampy tabletop, he excused himself out to Milwaukee's sleeping streets.

Outside he found College Kid puking onto a brick wall in a sort of strain that looked painful, like in an effort to relieve the pressure he accidentally built up more, and through the veins in his neck a fissure would open up and his face would explode into a million pieces. His eyes bulged, and Lorraine, who was leaning with him, kept a hand on his back in sympathy. She smoked something hand-rolled that Frank had never smelled before and appeared serene. "He okay?"

Lorraine puffed her humid mane with her free hand and then rested it across her waist. "He's an amateur. You responsible for him?"

"Never met the kid in my life," he chided. College Kid thought to himself how he did not appreciate that and would be dealing with Frank in the morning, if he survived the explosion. "Buffalo Springfield, huh? Not a wise choice."

"Some people don't appreciate good music," she said, taking a drag and fluttering her lashes.

"Your guitarist is a joke."

"Well that's just rude."

College Kid moaned, dug his fingernails into the wet grit between the bricks.

"Those chords were out of his league. Maybe he should consider a capo. Or another line of work." An interesting technique, emasculating the competition. "He's all thumbs up there. It's pathetic. He makes you look bad." Lorraine could only see him in silhouette, his shoulders were big enough to block out the little light coming in from the street. His voice chugged along slowly like a barge. She didn't know what he looked like exactly, but he was in uniform, smelled like a cross between Copenhagen and cinnamon candies, and he knew music enough to be critical. "And the way you dress. It makes you look like you don't have any tits."

Lorraine looked down at her bony chest. "I don't have any tits," a matter of fact. "Typical man. You criticize his ability, and my looks."

"I don't have anything to say about your ability," he responded. College Kid looked up from his stupor, watching his old buddy in action through crescent shaped slits. Frank stepped closer, she didn't move except to try to meet his eye. "I like your voice."

"I like your voice." She did. It felt like lava.

"What's with this hair?" He touched it like a grenade, not trusting it.

"Its spirit is free."

"Like yours?" he asked, putting his hand on her heart. Lorraine took one more drag and then stamped out whatever that stuff was under her wedge sandal. The fog rolling through the alley soaked into the asphalt, and the cork in her shoes was beginning to soak it up.

"Your hand is on my tit," she smiled with her eyes.

"What tit?" he asked, leaning in to kiss her. College Kid deflated down onto his knees, as though he had a chance up to then. Once again, another girl lost to Frank Gladney and his boyish allure.

Blow Torch

"Dinner was fantastic, Mark. Where did you learn to cook like that?" Aubergine hadn't seen a meal cooked by a person in years. She'd relaxed a bit, taken her hair down to reveal the curls that proved her relation to these other strangers in the room. Other than Mark, it was a room full of ringlets, like Shirley Temple had been doused in water and duplicates emerged from her back hair.

"The Cordon Bleu," using his best French accent. "In my younger years I thought I'd be a chef. But God had another plan."

"And what was that again?" Tim skepticized.

"Well, I was but a boy when Master Chef Mathieu," really punching that *U*, "told me I had a way with words. So here I am. A quotician." He leaned back in his chair and crossed an ankle onto his knee, quite satisfied with himself.

Tim cleared his throat. "A quotician." Had he heard right? Mark nodded modestly. "My bad, I'm not sure I know what a quotician does."

"Long story short, I dedicate my life to the study and creation of quotes and idiomatic phrases." He sipped his tea carefully, his lips protruding like a platypus.

"Pardon me for asking, Mark," Aubergine attempted, "but how does a quotician make a living?"

Mark nodded, used to this question. "A lot of speaking engagements, literary sound bites, speech writing, newspaper contributions, movie posters. Here and there you just sort of build a name for yourself. There's always someone looking for a catchphrase. Remember 'Show me the money?' That was me."

Aubergine narrowed her eyes. "You lost me."

"Movie posters?" Tim squeezed his eyebrows together, trying to eek out some understanding.

"He's very talented!" Bluebell intervened, petting her husband's arm like a spaniel.

Tim went concave into his chair, holding his untouched teacup in his left hand like an ornament. "So a dude tells you you're good with words, and instead of becoming, I don't know, a writer, or a poet, you spend your life coming up with quotes?"

Mark nodded. "A lot of my work includes the resurrection of old quotes, studying historical quoticians, not just writing my own."

Tim stroked his imaginary beard. "So you're a history buff who specializes in one-liners." Tim was doing everything in his power not to patronize Mark, but it always peeked through his words.

"He's very talented," Bluebell repeated, looking nervous. Maybe she was familiar with this line of questioning. "Honey, why not give them an example of some of your work."

"Apropos to today's rendezvous," Mark coughed into his hands and licked his lips, preparing to declare something genius. "A reunion is a party where everyone is the guest of honor."

"Yeah, I think I've heard that somewhere," Tim said dryly.

"It's a real job," Bluebell reassured the group. Luckily food fills any uncomfortable silence. "So who's ready for some crème brûlée?"

Mark assisted, unrattled by this very common reaction to his career. "I'll get the blow torch."

A minivan, a jamboree of four-year-olds, and now Mark was going to blow a French pie to smithereens.

Wilthon

Later in the evening Bluebell showed everyone to their sleeping quarters, which amounted to the pull-out couch in Mark's home office that Aubergine and Tim used to share when they were kids. "You get a lot of light coming in through that window, but other than that it's a pretty comfy little spot. And the bathroom is just down the hall by the kids. There are plenty of towels in the cabinet," she counted off her fingers, "if you need more toilet paper just look under the sink, there should be plenty of blankets but if you get chilly let me know and I'll bring some up from the basement-"

"We got it, Blue, go to bed," Auby reassured her, kissing her sister on the cheek. She smelled like vanilla.

"Okay. I love you," she said, a hand on both of her siblings' shoulders. "I'm so glad you're home." Her smile was genuine, maybe a little lonely. The crow's feet around her eyes doubled like sound waves when her happiness met melancholy in the middle.

Off Bluebell went to her bedroom, leaving the two in the hallway to make themselves comfortable. Auby gave her little brother the big eyes.

Tim spoke in a loud whisper, "Sissy, this is the creepiest thing I've ever seen in my life."

"It's not that bad."

"My lead singer once simulated an on-stage suicide using pig's blood, red Jell-O, and a machete. And this is weirder."

"Give her a break. In her world this is… normal."

Tim came in close to Auby, "These are the sorts of people with bodies in the basement."

"I highly doubt that. She's the one who said we could go down there to get extra blankets."

Tim gave her that. He always had a theory though that the more perfect a person appeared, the more they were hiding. Every squeaky clean baseboard represented to him a distress signal, like a flashlight beaming Morse code from a mountain top. "S.O.S." Save our Sissy. He sighed into his next criticism, "Have you seen her hair? Is that real?"

"Timmy, if I ever seek out Florence Henderhair, put me in an institution." The two laughed in a whisper when suddenly Tim was surprised by the presence of one of the indistinguishable W children. He quickly realized the kid had been hanging on their words from a nearby doorway.

"Shit, kid, what are you doing there? You should be in bed or something," shooing the W with his hands. But the kid didn't move. It was his house after all. "Which one are you?"

"Wilthon." From the angle Tim stood over him, Wilson's eyes were like moons and his mouth a glimmer of horizon.

"Kid, you're lurking. It's rude to lurk."

"You woke me up." Valid point. Tim and Auby might have owed him an apology. "Thum of uth are trying to thleep." And with that he turned away, stopping a second to add, "I like your panth." Wilson disappeared behind his door quietly so as not to wake the others.

"I'm in another dimension," Tim decided.

Aubergine giggled. "He likes your panth."

Cawcaw

"You should marry me while you can," Frank proclaimed void of any romance.

"While I can? Is there a line out the door I didn't notice?" Lorraine was naked, on her stomach, and Frank ran the back of two fingers down her side, riding the ridges of her ribs like train tracks. She jerked. "Don't. That tickles." He palmed her lower back and pulled her closer to him.

"I'm sure your mother would be impressed. Marrying a soldier."

"I think you're a little too impressed with yourself there, sir." Lorraine opened one eye to make sure he was listening, smiling just on the corner of her mouth that was showing. He got a chill and pulled the covers up over both of their heads. The only light between them was what little flecks of moon pierced the knit in the blanket. "Besides, my mother is long gone."

They'd only known each other a week, but still he expected to have known this by now. "She died?"

Lorraine laughed. "No. I don't think so anyway. Maybe." *Hopefully.*

"So what? You ran away or something?"

Lorraine flipped her head to the other side, preferring no eye contact for this part. A tuft of her hair fell over his eyes. "No. She did." She flipped back to face him, clearing his face of her curls. "And my dad's dead. So I guess that means you have no one to impress but me."

"Mission accomplished," he slapped her little bony butt, leaving a stinging hand print.

"Oh, please," she chuckled back at him. She had a noise to accompany her every reaction. A cawcaw for things she found preposterous, a nyipnyipnyip when she was feeling snarky, a gurdlygurdle high-pitched cackle when something surprised her, a croak for mild amusement.

"That laugh, Lorraine. You're so lucky you can sing. It makes it much easier to forget that god forsaken laugh." He teased her, but he meant it. He loved making her laugh, hated the inscrutability of whatever sound came out of her. She kissed his shoulder, looked up at him like a girl. He dug his hands in the back of her head, letting his fingers weave in and out of her curls like fabric. "I'm serious though, I should marry you."

"Yeah?" she traced a finger down his sideburn.

He shrugged, "If I don't, someone else will."

This was true. When Lorraine walked down the street, she caught every kind of look she could being the outcast. Lust, envy, pure hatred. She was special, like a spotlight following her from room to room. Frank loved it and stung with paranoia all together in one delicious sandwich.

What Lorraine wasn't revealing, because she was good at hiding her hand, was that she'd never been to bed with anyone else, certainly never spent three days with her clothes off, and the free spirit in her was only so free. He unleashed that something sensual she'd kept trapped under her politics for too long, and he had her heart. She'd never tell him, never in their 38 years together. She always wanted him to remember she could walk away at any time. She could, but would never.

Frank shipped out a month later, just two days after their wedding. She wore white eyelet and carried wildflowers they picked along the way. He wore his dress uniform. The only guests were a judge and a college kid named Tim.

Lorraine

Bluebell's Astro Van sped down the I-94 at a good 80 miles per hour, spiriting the siblings out to Waukesha where Mother lived. Despite the temperature, Tim rolled down a window and shut his eyes, letting the November chill numb his face. Numb is always better than fear. The wind whipping around his head kind of made him feel like he was hovering over the edge of the Grand Canyon, a gust away from sailing down onto a rock. This image was less unsettling than their destination.

"So when was the last time either of you saw Mother?" Bluebell cheeped, fully energized.

Tim glared out at the world zipping by. "When I left." Bluebell knew that damn well.

"Um, I'm going to say five or six years ago. Right when my album came out. I remember because that's when her mailed stopped," a blessing and a curse considering Mother's rare ability to write a sneer into her letters. Any conversation about her since they were kids was a series of subtle digs volleyed against guilt trips. Auby would write songs about her mother issues, and Bluebell would say, "thank goodness Mother passed that talent down to you."

Bluebell worked the numbers, "Auby, that was eight years ago. Maybe nine. I know because it was right after Mark and I got married. Your album came out, and he said 'Our soundtrack is finally born.' Isn't that sweet?" Her siblings rolled their eyes in sync. Bluebell glared into her rearview mirror at her sister. "He sold that one for $200."

Tim squinched his forehead, still unable to accept Mark's career was real.

The further the trio made it West the more lush the trees, and Aubergine marveled over the colors. She missed this, she had to admit, stared at every last one, felt a twinge of inspiration from the rare red tree among the golds and greens. Back at Bluebell's house the trees were all bare, possibly because such proximity to Lake Michigan had blown in strong enough to shake them loose. Out here there was still a hint of fall left, like going back in time.

Mother Gladney lived in a turn of the century old two-story, which century nobody could quite pinpoint, that at closer inspection was nearing dilapidation. From the road it looked like a perfectly maintained relic, especially among the refurbished treasures sitting adjacent. Up close the front gate swung freely in the breeze, the latch gone and yawing just enough it couldn't be secured if it wanted to be. The siding had been painted and repainted enough that chips in the surface revealed a rainbow of years past. Yellow for Bluebell's graduation, Red the year Aubergine married and divorced in a month's time, Purple the year Tim was born. Like a mood house. Some things hadn't changed; the grass had been cut but not trimmed, and the weeds overtook just about every surface. Mother cited Survival of the Fittest and defended them fiercely to critics.

The van sat in park. All three siblings paused to breathe before opening their doors.

Aubergine asked what she'd been putting off the whole ride over. "Alright, Blue, what are we in for here? Is she," swallowing, "*normal?*"

"For her, you mean?"

Tim got a shiver. "I have to be honest, guys. I'm not even sure I have an accurate memory of her. When I try to envision her face, an image of one of those wind-up monkeys and the cymbals pops into my head. *Clank! Clank! Clank!* You know?" They knew. Indeed it had been long enough he wasn't sure if the persona in his mind wasn't just a trumped up caricature of his mother. Maybe she wasn't that bad. Maybe he confused fleeing the evil of this home with basic American youth rebellion.

Resigning to their fate, Bluebell killed the ignition but left the keys inside, as if setting them up for a quick get-away. Like a rag-tag army all three stepped out of the vehicle and walked the front steps, scanning the neighborhood for any surprise attacks. They wouldn't put it past mother to pop out of the bushes like a live-action garden gnome, or fall from the sky like a dead bird. Mother made entrances even after she'd already entered, as if to say "Here I am, and don't you fucking forget it."

As they neared the front door, lined up like a firing squad, a faint melody could be heard through the door, their mother was singing. Tim squinted to hear better. It was Simon and Garfunkel. Before they could so much as knock, the song grew louder and the door swung open with all the enthusiasm in the world, and she sung her welcome.

"Parsley," her hand over where a heart would be, "Sage," nodding to Tim, "Rosemary," to Bluebell, and "Thyyyyme," to Aubergine. Perfect pitch, even after all these years. Her white hair was bundled atop her head in a sort of origami, topped off with a rhinestone brooch she'd repurposed to keep it all perilously held together. "Greetings, my long lost darlings. Well, not all of you are so long or lost," gripping Bluebell's hands with her own, gazing intensely into her wayward children's eyes. They froze, emotions in a holding pattern, at least on the surface.

Mother turned to Aubergine first, saving Tim for last, perhaps still deciding on which arrows to sling his way.

"My second born. We considered calling you Serendipity." Auby had heard this story a million times, however never in a proud story to houseguests or neighbors. Mother had her own take. "Nope, you weren't supposed to happen." *Put that on a bumper sticker*, Aubergine thought to herself. "But because of you, Father and I stayed together. You saved our marriage." She always was great at putting a positive spin on "staying together for the kids."

Mother's gestures were fluid, like a spirit floating near them, punctuated by random grabs, theatrical pointing, a shaky fist in the air. "And here you are before me, a celebrity. How nice of you to make time for your deceased father. Is this genuine affection or just research for a memoir?" The ending of her words hung like a stink in the air, the R disappearing behind that dramatic "mem-wahhh."

Anyone else would have answered that question, but her children were familiar enough with her approach to know this was rhetorical. Everything was rhetorical, and no one was ever quick enough to respond before her next attack. Rapid fire, like her thoughts ran on a wheel while her mouth spit out lead. Mother didn't speak to be spoken to, she spoke to be feared.

"And Timothy," Aubergine exhaled through her mouth, temporarily off the hook. Tim's posture was steadfast, he'd let go of pleasing anyone from about birth. "How was your college graduation? My sincerest apologies for not being able to attend such an historic occasion, where yet another of the Gladney success stories took root. Ah, wait," bringing a finger to her lips, "I'm confusing you with someone else's child. Where *did* you graduate from?

Because we all know it wasn't secondary school." Tim didn't remove his hands from his pockets, just waited for this to pass, like a kidney stone. "Please, come in," she said, stepping aside to clear an entry for them. "I want to hear all about your fascinating path to greatness. Let's start with your Nobel Prize and work backward, shall we?"

Bluebell, used to it, walked in without hesitation. The others exchanged an I-will-if-you-will and grimly made their way forward.

"You move like tree sap," Mother pronounced, then shut the door behind her. "Dare I confuse you with Olympians."

In this home of sorts, the grown children felt a combination of claustrophobia and awe with the décor Mother had amassed since their escape. Over the mantle three urns held the dusty remains of God knows whom, not Father, who presently awaited eternal rest patiently on a slab somewhere. As many surfaces as possible were covered in velvet or lace, everything else hard wood or stained glass. Small animals were mounted on the wall, skunks, a bat, an eagle, a badger, whose head Mother had adorned with a renaissance style flowered wreath. "Some of these have to be illegal," Auby murmured.

Tim felt like the armadillo's eyes were following him. "She always did love dead shit." It smelled like old books, it always did. He remembered visiting a palm reader with a pothead old girlfriend of his and feeling in it the familiarity of this room. He remarked at the time that it felt like his mother was "still with him," then realized she wasn't dead yet, and thus this palm reader simply shared an affinity for butt-ugly furniture.

In a curio cabinet Mother had collected vintage opium pipes, angel figurines, beer cans from the 1940s, and one framed, grainy photo of her great-great-grandfather standing with his beloved steer in the middle of a Wisconsin pasture. Her brand of crazy dated way back before Wisconsin had a name, the photo would suggest. A cuckoo clock chimed one solitary cuckoo, despite there being at least twenty of them ticking and clicking from every possible corner of the room. Tim checked his watch. It was 11:17.

"You going to sit down or just stand there admiring my antiques?" Mother was in what was always her favorite chair, a mauve wingback with a giant lace doily draped over the back. Everyone knew that doily was actually a Christmas tree skirt, but she found it on sale, and this woman was the master of finding marked down merchandise and assuming its purpose.

Bluebell came in from the kitchen with a makeshift tray, known in most homes as a cutting board, carrying coffee and fixings, as though she'd done this a million times at Mother's place. Aubergine felt an immediate disdain for the fact that not only was her sister comfortable in this tomb, but she knew enough where the cream and sugar were kept to have them materialize before they could even remove their coats.

The siblings sat where they could, for there was only a loveseat and a coffee table available to choose from, other than the floor. A small dining chair sat in the corner, but there was a stuffed cat "sleeping" on it, and since Auby couldn't tell if it was once living or just an uncanny replica, she opted for the table. This happened to be the most appropriate seat in the house for her, suggesting subliminally that she was ready to go at any time. It was important she communicate this sentiment to her mother at every opportunity, that she wasn't getting too comfortable, since she was all of 12 years old.

Bluebell poured coffee for the room. "Mother makes the best coffee, you guys. Organic beans from, where, Mother?" Bluebell always skirted the tension.

"Humboldt."

Tim snickered.

"Alright, Tim, since you're so in need of all the attention today," which was a clear misread on her part, "why don't you start by telling me where you've been for ten years?" He was surprised she'd kept track. He assumed she'd spent the last ten years burning the photos she never took of him. "Are you still smoking marijuana? I'm not judging. I just want to know if I should hide my valuables." Tim didn't respond, just smiled, daring her. "This is an artistic get-up you've put together for yourself. Either you're a musician or a homosexual prostitute. Well? Which is it?"

"You guessed it, Mother. I fuck for money."

Bluebell blanched. It had been years since she heard the F-word with such verve or frequency.

"He speaks! Well, high-dee-ho, all it took was calling him a fag to provoke him. I thought for sure I'd have to drag out *your* failed career," casting a quick look and insensitive reference to Aubergine. Back to Tim, "So when did you lose your accent?"

"Around Iowa."

"Well, you sound like a vagrant." Mother's hands trembled. She seemed older than most mothers. She emoted with every possible limb, whether or not she had the energy.

"Would you stop picking on him?" Aubergine had had it. "You've been trying to sound like an aristocrat since before he was even born. Now that's enough. This isn't how you greet people."

Growing up in Mother's household was a filtered version of this, and it was as if she'd saved up insults for every breath they were gone. These kids knew what they were in for by meeting, and it was on a level comical to listen to, the ravings of an aging lunatic. On the other hand it was genuine. This batty old lady wasn't confusing them with their drunken uncle or the slutty teenager who delivered her pizza. No, it was truth she dreamed up laying in the bathtub, driving down the road, vacuuming the rug, stewing in her silence and plotting this exact script. For ten years Mother had developed an opinion about everything, except their achievements.

She turned her attention to the middle child. "Fine, fine. I'm done pouting. I missed my children, what can I tell you." The room sank in silence as Mother lit a Camel. "Aubergine, I read in one of those magazines with the movie stars on the cover that you're marrying someone famous again. Who was it again? Simon…Clooney…or Douglas…or something like that."

"That was two years ago, Mother."

"Well, that was the last time anyone's written anything about you, what else do I have to go off of?" She waited for a reaction. "And your career? Have you come out of retirement?"

"I wouldn't call it a retirement. I just took some time off to redirect things." Three minutes in and

Aubergine was already defending herself. Tim cringed, knowing it was better not to humor Mother with explanations. It gives her all the power. "It's the equivalent of someone going back to school to get their Master's."

"Yes. Just like that. Except without an education. Or job prospects."

Aubergine huffed. "Can we just get to the details? Why are we here? Bluebell, you dragged us along, now why don't you convince me to stay?"

Bluebell put down her coffee gently and straightened her blouse. "You're right. We're avoiding the real issue. Father has a plot set aside for himself in Prairie Home Cemetery. Mother says it's a nice, shady little spot right in between his old band mates. Remember them? Roscoe and Floyd?"

"Well thank God. I thought for sure we were going to find him stuffed around here somewhere," Tim muttered sarcastically.

Bluebell realized just then, "Mother, if there's no room by Father, where will we put you one day?"

Mother patted Bluebell's hand, "Not to worry. When my time comes I've decided to walk into nature and let my body be absorbed by the soil."

"Like an old dog," Tim added.

"Father didn't want that for himself, and I respect that." She did not in fact. "It was till death do we part, not decomposition." All faces in the room winced. "So it's all fairly simple. We'll meet here Wednesday morning at eight, and that's Wisconsin time, not Hollywood big-wig time. You show up on time or we're leaving without you.

You miss this train, and you're walking, you hear me?" All nodded. "You'll all be expected to say a few words-"

"Whoa, whoa, whoa," Tim put on the brakes, gesturing furiously along with Aubergine.

Bluebell shushed them. "I know, I know. Calm down." She adjusted herself and faced Mother, advocating for her spiteful siblings. "What could they possibly say about Father? They haven't seen him in ten years."

"I'm happy to stand up and there and talk about what I remember about him. How about that?" Tim fumed. "Maybe a poem? What's my time limit? Because I could write a whole sonnet about that bastard."

"Just because you had your differences, I see no reason why you can't come up with something compassionate. You're the creative type." Mother appeared to be oblivious to the reality of their childhood.

"Yes, we had our differences. He was a dick, I kept my head down. What's there to say?"

"Just say what people say at funerals."

"So, lie?" he asked.

"Lord in heaven, is it so hard to come up with one good quality?" Mother wasn't getting it, even if she of all people saw his decline down into a drunk and angry martyr from her front row seat.

Aubergine threw up her hands in frustration. Mother was certainly an eccentric, held a skewed view of the world where ridicule built character, abuse was a gift, and always found a way to understand the man no one else did. This was her finest and worst quality, something she claimed proved her enlightenment, accepting Frank for all that he was. It also distinguished her from those other mothers at school. Aubergine remembered the mom next door and her attendance at every recital, and remembered her own mother and her insistence on attending a coven meeting instead, whatever that was, the day Auby started her period and hadn't any clue what to do with a tampon. Bluebell was off in college with her own problems, and had no idea Lorraine's maternal expression of female solidarity was to light some incense and pray to the four elements. Aubergine's early teen years rode the same rails as her mother's Wiccan phase.

"I'm outta here," she declared and looked around for her purse, not realizing she'd never taken it off her arm. "Sissy, I'm walking if you're not coming with me."

"Well shit, don't leave without me," Tim said, lumbering up from the loveseat. Mother leaned back, rested her chin in her palm, and smiled too knowingly for their liking.

As the two scuttled out the door, wiping dust from their bottoms, Bluebell attempted a polite goodbye and a kiss on Mother's cheek, rushing out to meet her siblings at the family truckster. Mother was motionless, mute, and satisfied, like one of her very own mounted vermin.

The Chicken and the Egg

The Astro Van was mostly quiet except for
Bluebell's attempts at finding a country station that wasn't
on a commercial. She needed some noise, and she needed it
now. Aubergine finally pounded the power button off,
staring at her sister in embittered disbelief. Bluebell
resigned to the road, doing what she did, avoiding.

"Well, I have to hand it to you, Sissy. Best. Trip.
Ever." Tim pumped a half-hearted, sarcastic fist into the air
in solidarity. Bluebell didn't appreciate any of it and kept
her eyes on the road. "So let me get this straight. You drive
at mach speed to get to Mother's, but 55 to get home? What
the fuck is wrong with this picture?"

"Don't provoke me, Auby," Bluebell pointed to the
crucifix again, her full time job the last couple of days.

"That's like breaking into prison," Aubergine
jabbed.

"I'm not interested today." Bluebell tried to tune her
sister out.

Tim bobbed his head to an invisible beat in his
mind, opting out. It soothed him. As a kid he would bob
and Frank and Lorraine used to speculate that he was
probably just a little retarded.

"How can you go to that woman's home and,"
dramatically, "*serve her coffee*? How dirty does that make
you feel? You're like Hitler's maid." Bluebell reached for

the radio's power button, gently moving the volume to background music. "What is the purpose in us being here? Seriously. I'm really asking you. What were you trying to get out of this?" Bluebell edged the music up a hair. "Who gives a shit that Father's dead? I mean, really," rolling down the window, yelling at passing cars, "is anyone losing sleep over this?!" Bluebell didn't budge. Steely eyes on the road. "Whose funeral do you want to swing by after Father's? How about the Unabomber? I can whip up a eulogy for that little fiesta, too."

Bluebell responded by cranking the volume at full blast, tightening her mouth into a wrinkly little coin purse, looking just like Mother. Aubergine responded by yanking the volume knob as hard as she could, a twist this way, then the other, until the knob ripped off completely into her hands. The van weaved and swayed on its axles as Bluebell reacted, shocked by this blatant vandalism, struggling to turn the music off with just the nub that remained. Auby considered the knob for a second and then threw it out the window into the oblivion on the freeway shoulder. The van steadied, all were silent.

"You owe me a knob," Bluebell said coarsely, trying to get her breath.

Aubergine inhaled, chose her words. "Bluebell, you need to understand me on this. Father was someone different to us." She looked straight ahead, fortified herself, done crying years and years ago. "He took care of you. But we don't know that guy."

Bluebell drove on, remembering the years before Aubergine and Tim came along, when it was her, a sweet child with clothes that matched, an artistic mother who sang "Carolina On My Mind" at the top of her lungs to hear herself over the vacuum, a quiet but genius father who only communicated to dole out compliments or sing lullabies, dinners together, making her parents laugh by telling Richard Pryor jokes she didn't understand even as she told them, singing "This Land is Your Land" so many times one day all the words mushed together into one big melodic nebula, practicing handstands against the wall hoping Father would walk buy and tickle her pits, spilling Mother's perfume and giggling as Lorraine said, "Quick, rub your neck in the carpet before it all goes to waste," then collapsing into her arms as Mother said, "At first laying down, as a fact fundamental, that nothing with God can be accidental." Bluebell spent her whole childhood riding on Mother's recall for perfectly appropriate literary quotes.

Where did those quotes go? Where was Mother's joy? The Egg, her parents' zest drying up into a shrivel, the Chicken her siblings and all the blame they placed on others for their own self pity. This was a riddle she couldn't figure out, no matter how many peaceful drives she took, Sundays spent in church, shopping carts she pushed as the Ws' collective babbling and screams took on a numbing white noise. The blame shifted with the seasons, and it was never enough to say "it takes two" and lay the responsibility a little on everyone. In Bluebell's very black and white world, where right and wrong were distinctive, she needed to figure out finally who started this mess, like insurance that the pattern could not be repeated.

The quest for the origin of her family's dysfunction resulted in Bluebell's overly structured life, and in effect, her own dysfunction. There was no escape. It only dawned on her in that instant. She was the end of the road of a perfectly designed chain reaction. A + B = C. And no matter how hard she tried, the answer would never be D. She would always be a little bit obsessive, never have enough structure, never enough control. Because that was her place in the equation. She was C. Damn it, she was C. And that deflated her.

Nearing home, Bluebell's little pocket of stability where her picturesque Victorian waited for her, the van finally rested at a stoplight. Tim looked out the window and made an executive decision. Just as the light turned green he reached for the door handle and slid the door wide open, stepping out into traffic. Cars behind them feared laying on their horns, partly because of Midwestern virtue, partly because they weren't used to that much black clothing in the 'burbs. This prejudice worked in his favor from time to time, on this occasion allowing him to halt traffic on a busy street in an entitled neighborhood.

Tim waved his sisters off and ran over to the Forty Winks Inn sitting adjacent from the van. A semi-sterile motel room with four white walls and bad local art seemed like a big warm hug by comparison at that moment. Impulse equaled gut wisdom, according to Tim's old soul.

Dusty Hearts

"Ka-help-yuh?" the gentleman behind the counter mumbled, looking down his Lennon specs at this leather-bound guest.

"Yeah," Tim considered the rates posted on the wall and reached for his wallet. "What if I only need twenty winks?"

Lennon-specs squinted, then widened his eyes as far as they would go, moving his glasses to his forehead. "Tim Gladney," he said breathlessly, like he'd discovered a new planet.

Tim eyeballed this stranger suspiciously. "That's me."

"It's me, dude," patting his man-tits, taking a step back to do a spin.

"No shit, Percy Kaczynski." *Fantastic.*

"In the flesh," lots of flesh as it turned out. Since playing guitar together in the ninth grade, old Percy had packed on about a million pounds. And he reeked of beer.

Tim reached out for a handshake. "Nice to see you. You look great, man." Percy did not look great, man.

"Nah, I've aged about a hundred years. Got a kid. You go gray like *that*," he said, snapping his fingers. "How about you? Where you been, old Glad-Bag?" Tim never understood that nickname, maybe because his family never had a TV and therefore no commercials, and certainly never name-brand trash bags, if they had trash bags at all. Once Lorraine lined the can with crunchy leaves, claiming they absorbed the smell. They did not, however. "I heard you were in fuckin' Canada and shit."

"Portland, actually."

"That's right. I had it backwards. Maine's dope."

Tim thought about correcting him, but decided better of it under the rare but frightening possibility Percy would one day be passing though Oregon needing someone to help him score some weed. "So how about a room? Sorry about my lame joke."

"Nah, man, it's cool. You and every other fuckin' guy who walks in this place says it, except your delivery was spectacular." Percy punched a few keys intensely into the computer. "T-I-M-G-L-A-D, it's still Gladney, right? You didn't get married?" Percy asked inexplicably, and Tim found no urge to clarify, still hoping to pay the twenty-wink rate on account of their friendly history.

Tim shook his head.

"Alrighty, homes. Hang on, let me just work some fucking web magic here." Abruptly Percy snapped into posture. "I can't believe I forgot to ask. How's that hot sister of yours? I always knew that girl would get famous. I should have been nicer to her." As though his ignoring her all together rendered their true love unrequited.

Tap tap tap tap tap tap on the keys... "But if you think about it, she isn't even really famous anymore, you know? She's barely even out of my league." Tim thought for a moment how horrified by that point of view Aubergine would be upon hearing it. "Where's she been?"

Percy leaned over the counter, looking Tim square in the eyes, usurping the recipient's response to all the questions he'd just asked. "You know what she needs. She needs an image 'make-over,'" using air quotes, "because the problem is her fans don't know who the fuck she is. Is she a pop star? Is she a country singer? Shit, dude. Is she schizoid or somethin'?" Percy laughed at his own joke in a way that rippled across his face and down his jowls. "You tell her when she flip-flops like that she loses credibility with her public."

Tim nodded, wondered when his sister ever possessed credibility in her entire life. On her first album cover a little bit of her nipple was showing, which a sleazy exec surely noticed but pretended not to. That sold a million in about the length of a sneeze. She lip synched the Star Spangled Banner at the Super Bowl, forgetting to spit out her gum, thus peeving every American who owned a TV set, and many who didn't, including Lorraine Gladney. To be fair, she was really drunk at the time. And though she wrote all her own music, her toppest of top hits rhymed "summer's day" with "bay-bay." Tim believed in her, knew she had been seduced by the music business machine, and that anything she had in her worth a damn was suppressed by the record company as being too edgy, dark, or smart.

Still, when she left the pop world, paid for a retreat in rehab despite having no addiction to speak of, and reemerged "healthy," the folk album Aubergine always dreamed of producing never surfaced. Instead she came out twanging, and a new desperate genre was born: Bluegrass Pop. The family joke goes that when *Dusty Hearts* was released, musicians everywhere aged eleven minutes, one listen of her album being one minute more dangerous than smoking a cigarette.

Dusty Hearts never rose beyond number six on the Billboard charts, and Aubergine's meteoric rise and fall became a caricature of itself. A starlet interviewed in *Vanity Fair* feared making the wrong moves in this industry, of "pulling an Aubergine." Occasionally Tim got a call in the middle of the night, her only sibling in the same time zone and on the same schedule. They talked about music, she gave him lyrics when he was stuck, suggested time changes in his latest composition, laid back and listened while he sat down his receiver and played for her whatever he was working on, anything, and fell asleep, like when they were kids. The thunk-thunk of his boots keeping time to his song felt strangely intimate, like their own secret conversation down through the floorboards, riding the San Andreas Fault up under her bed or couch or wherever she found herself that particular night. This was the safe zone. Not career, not family, not bull riders. Just music. He asked no tough questions, and neither did she.

"How come your sister didn't Osmond you, man?" Percy slid a form for him to sign across the counter.

"Osmond me?"

"You know. Keep it in the family. Take you to Hollywood and make you fuckin' famous. You coulda been lying in a bed of coke and strippers by now. Damn, dude. Missed that train, know what I'm sayin'?" Tim didn't. The last stripper he had near him smelled of gasoline, and he found the whole naked thing very unsettling, far too personal to be happening in public. The coke though, there was a time in his life an unending supply of cocaine might have been mighty nice. Too nice. He felt lucky to have gone undiscovered, and therefore too poor for coke, during such dark days.

Fat Percy worked some numbers, ran Tim's card, and once he was gone called every one of their high school friends to let them know Aubergine Gladney's brother was in town, and he looked like shit.

The gods

Initially when Frank came home from the war, all was how he'd hoped it to be.

What no one really told him was that the world would change without him. Suns rose and set, people got sick, got married, politicians took reign, all basic seasons of change he didn't seem to realize when he was away. It all existed before him, it existed without him. Coming home to hyper reality can be unsettling to a soldier who has spent a tour on what can only be considered another planet trapped in time.

But Frank was realistic. He knew Lorraine was an unorthodox woman who could be sucked down whatever rabbit hole was the sparkliest and in view. He could come home to a dope-head, someone who burned bras, however symbolically (since she owned none), an angry protestor maybe. Frank saw the direction the world was heading years before, he knew decorum was on its way out of fashion. Marrying Lorraine was an effort to hang on to whatever was still and reliable left in his pin-tip of the world. To have something of his own to cling to when he returned who would incorporate him back in the fold would be his saving grace.

Luckily when he walked in the door, she wasn't holding a joint, not at that moment anyway. She wasn't reading *the Feminine Mystique* to a room full of hairy women, or drawing in big black letters onto a placard the words "Draft Beer, Not Boys." When he opened the door, he caught her in profile slumped over a drafting table with a pencil in her mouth, an acoustic draped over her lap. The sound of his footsteps upset her focus. She wasn't expecting anybody, and here was her husband, fifteen feet from her, and not in Vietnam.

There she is. Right where I left her, Frank thought to himself. Like he'd found his missing keys. "Lorrainey, you have to lock the door in this neighborhood. I thought we went over this."

She cupped her hand over her mouth for a bit longer than she could help, containing whatever emotion she could that didn't squeeze out from behind it. The air left her lungs like a vacuum. The guitar disappeared, the pencil dropped out of her mouth and before she knew it she was in his arms, her legs wrapped around his waist like a chimpanzee. He held her tight and sunk his face down into her collar.

"Jesus Christ, Frank," she said, muffled, her mouth buried into his body.

They rocked and embraced until her legs got tired and she let herself down from his branches. Lorraine still couldn't speak. An hour before she was sewing a new hem onto a skirt, humming a tune, making plans to visit Bradford Beach. Now the husband she barely knew or remembered stood in her doorway. She still wore her wedding ring though. Modest as it was, likely not even real gold, it was still what she put on her finger the day she signed that contract a year before.

He stared down at her, looking for anything he didn't recognize. She looked older. He couldn't believe what a year of whatever life she'd been living had done to the topography of her face. Lines existed where they hadn't. A palm reader could trace one wrinkle from the eye out to the jaw line and call it her "nights wondering where Frank is line," another one around the corner of her mouth and call it her "how am I going to make the bills line," one straight horizontal across her forehead and call it the "political and social unrest line," and say they were all very long and pronounced and she was destined for a burdensome life. Indeed Lorraine looked at herself in pictures and compared them to her reflection and adjusted the lighting, added makeup, anything to try and match the breeziness of the apparition in the photo.

"You didn't write me once," Lorraine said to her husband, stepping away from his noticeably shrunken frame. She wasn't going to let him hug her out of her disapproval, at least not at this moment. He would have to explain himself before she would accept him back into this Ferris wheel of her life.

"Don't you know? Don't you know I was here waiting for you? I prayed. I prayed and I prayed." A single frizz jutted out from her temple like antennae. Frank chose to focus on that while he grit his teeth.

"And I prayed some more, Frank. First I prayed to all the gods, every god I could think of. I prayed to the Catholic God, and the Baptist God, and the Lutheran God. I looked up Nordic gods and prayed to them. I looked up Oriental gods, thinking there might be such a thing. So guess what," she pointed to figurines she'd positioned around the apartment that pretty much had her covered in any religion- Buddhas everywhere, pictures of the Pope, a totem pole or two, a Star of David hanging from a lamp, a large Zeus candle that she didn't dare burn, "now I'm apparently a religious fanatic. A zealot." In her pre-Frank life, she'd have considered this a personal insult.

"Then someone told me Vietnamese people don't believe in any of that, and there were no gods watching over you over there, that you were your own gods. So that was a month of crying right there. But I kept praying, and praying, and praying. Then I stopped praying for your safety and just begged that you come home. Then I stopped begging you to come home, and I started just asking for a letter. Anything with your handwriting on it. Or a fingerprint. Anything. Then I stopped checking the mailbox at all. I'd wait until it was spilling over, because I couldn't face the disappointment again and again."

She waited. Frank still had nothing and everything to say. He didn't know whether to yell and scream at her, shove her through a wall for all her selfishness, to illuminate her to what he was doing while she was bypassing the mailbox, *because Lorrainey, it wasn't pretty*. Or whether he wanted just to tear her clothes off and absorb right into her body instead, let all of his weight down on top of her, make every kind of ugly face he could make to show her he loved her, let their sweat mix into a sort of soup in her belly button, bruise each other with too much grabbing, hip bones on flesh, and arise from it with bite marks and mysterious aches they didn't remember the source of. The sun rose and set while he was gone, Lorraine got the flu twice, went stag to three of her high school friends' weddings, voted Humphrey, but the world didn't spin so far as to erase the month they'd spent together before he left. That still very much remained, and despite the hell in her face, she still had that one curl standing up out of her head, that bony chest staring back at him like chainmail. Still he couldn't speak, couldn't move.

"So now that I've given up, now that I've completely given myself over to whatever the hell is going to happen to you, this is when you show up? I woke up today and the first thing I said to myself was that I was too tired. I'm just too tired to feel anything anymore. I made a list of things I was going to do," she grabbed a scribbled list from the drafting table, "just to keep one foot in front of the other today. And here you are. I can't tell if all that praying was for nothing, or if this is exactly what I asked for." Lorraine was exasperated, winded. Her shoulders collapsed forward.

Frank set down his big green bag and slid it to the corner, trying not to disturb the disorder that he knew was arranged precisely as she wanted it. He stepped to her slowly, an obvious limp he was trying to dampen by smiling and at least giving the appearance of not being in pain from. But it hurt. It hurt like hell. She could tell, and her face fell. Her forehead and cheeks imploded like a crumpled piece of paper, and the tears dropped faster than she could choke them back. His reality finally came to her.

Lorraine leaned into his chest face first and inhaled him- still tobacco and cinnamon- and he gripped her head and neck with his great big hands. Then, on cue, from a corner of the room, underneath a sweet yellow blanket, a baby giggled.

Frank lurched away from her, like she'd adopted a pit bull while he was away.

Lorraine grinned with all her teeth, and the tears dried instantly. She wiped her face and put her hands in her pockets. "She's got my laugh."

Mush

That night Mark simmered some white wine in
a large braising pan with a few pats of butter, shallots, and
thinly sliced garlic. The girl W stirred air in a large mixing
bowl, mimicking Daddy's whisking as best a four year old
could. Mark removed four fat Cornish game hens from the
fridge that had been slathered and stuffed and injected with
herbs and more butter and were awaiting their hot tub orgy
with the shallots and garlic. Aubergine found the whole
meal very sexy, all slippery and fragrant, and the concept of
ripping meat off the bone excited her in the most primal
way. She was beginning to understand the appeal of this
domestic living.

"Aubergine, have you ever tried real French bread?
As in prepared by a French woman?
Mark talked with the serrated knife like it was an extra
appendage, waving it around for emphasis.

"A woman? Not a man?" Bluebell challenged.
"You're a cook, too, you know."

"No man can make bread like a woman. It's
chauvinistic, but also a compliment. I think it's in the
knuckles, all that kneading." He winked at his woman.

"I don't think I have," Auby liked this side of him.
No wisdom, just a tour of the world moving through her
nose. Every so often he treated the family to all his skill, a
full-scale operation involving rolled up sleeves and a
cracked window. Sometimes the neighbors would call and

ask what that smell was. He would say "something I just whipped up," even though it required a shirt change before service so as not to alert the family to the arduousness of four French courses. Guilt was not a side dish. He wanted them all to enjoy his work purely and without worry for his trouble.

"I hope this meal doesn't actually taste like sweat," he joked, wiping his forehead with a length of sleeve. "I kid. Family is worth it. And it's not often we get celebrities at our table." Aubergine had begun to hate that word over the last couple of days. But unlike most people, he meant this and was humbled by her presence. When Bluebell informed him of her visit, he fully expected she'd be staying at the Pfister downtown, not on the pull-out upstairs, sleeping under their retired duvets.

Bluebell cooed, "Don't sell yourself short, Mister. Aubergine, did you know Mark was recently featured on the WTMJ Channel 4 News?"

"I did not."

Bluebell beamed proudly, "Yep, he was speaking at the Nicolet High School commencement and the news truck was there, and the next thing he knew they were interviewing him for a full four minute segment. Four minutes!"

"Four minutes?" Aubergine asked.

Mark assured her, "That's kind of a lot."

"Well, would ya look at that," Aubergine bloomed. It was no Teen's Choice Award, but cool for a guy like him. She understood that accolades were relative, and fully appreciated the momentousness of this one.

"What did you say they used as the sound bite?"
Bluebell asked.

"I said,

> A brief candle; both ends burning
> An endless mile; a bus wheel turning
> A friend to share the lonesome times
> A handshake and a sip of wine
> So say it loud and let it ring
> We are all a part of everything
> The future, present and the past
> Fly on proud bird
> You're free at last.

The kids loved it. The parents thought it was too mature.
But hey," shrugging, "you play to your audience."

Aubergine reached for a pen. "A candle? Burning at
both ends? How'd that go?"

"Oh, I didn't write that one. That's an old Charlie
Daniels line. He wrote it on the way to his friend's funeral.
Such a poetic story, really." Aubergine acquiesced, the
song already existed. "So I suppose it's about death, but I
kind of like to think it's about the future, and freedom, but
also a tie to where we come from. It's beautiful."

Aubergine nodded, processing that point.

Suddenly the three remaining Ws shuffled in the
room, their noses red and snotty. Bluebell quickly attended
to them, a good mom, removing coats, hanging fuzzy caps
and mittens onto the midget-sized hat rack, rubbing little
hands between hers and blowing her heart and soul's heat

down in between them, as if this was her daily routine. Aubergine watched and admired.

"Now explain to me who is a twin? Because they all look pretty identical."

"Triplets, actually. Fraternal. Wilson is the oldest, almost five," Bluebell held him by the head and he stood patiently like he'd been through this before. "And about two months after he came, I was pregnant with the other three."

"Irish twins," Aubergine explained.

"Qua-rupleths," Wilson corrected.

Aubergine felt the weight of her guilt like a cinderblock tied to her ankle. She'd spent so many years in Los Angeles, or else on the road, or else dodging Bluebell's calls, she had no idea her sister had triplets just a few years before. This was something reality TV shows were made of, and yet Aubergine only knew of two pregnancies occurring, not the final count of her offspring. For some reason in her memory the pregnancies were further apart, but then when she thought back to those five years of fame, that was a hazy time in general. Too much happening at once, and for what? To miss the birth, to completely fail to acknowledge the birth of four children in one year? The razzmatazz of her Hollywood life seemed so small now that she was in this kitchen with all these little descendents of hers.

Goodness knows where their family Christmas photos had gone all those years. Aubergine's personal assistant sorted the mail and had a slash and burn attitude toward the process, shredding anything that wasn't a glamorous invite. Fan mail went unanswered, family milestones unacknowledged. A whole world passed by her while she was deciding between hair extensions or a new tattoo as her latest development that kept the tabloids interested. Her eyes welled remembering these innumerably empty moments in her life. "I don't know where you two get the energy."

Mark smiled, "They're all so close in age, we just wind them up and let them go. We're pretty lucky that they all came when they did, because there isn't a lot of that birth order nonsense. They can just be who they are and entertain each other."

Wendy poked Watson in the eye with the lip-gloss she found in Aubergine's purse, which she'd opened, and so a red smudge streaked across Watson's eyelid. "Ouch!" he yelped, as Bluebell yanked it from her hands and sent her to the corner. She didn't even need to say the words. Wendy saw Bluebell's face and knew she'd failed this little test of her boundaries, and quietly she slunk to her usual spot.

"That's not to say they don't almost kill each other every day." Wendy whimpered with her big lower lip. "Everything is an implement in this house. We had to take William to the emergency room a few months back. Wendy smashed a light bulb over his head. A compact fluorescent."

Aubergine twitched at that thought, "Aren't those things loaded with, I don't know, toxic shit?"

"Yeah, well." Bluebell sighed. All in a day's work. "Wilson drank Windex once. Another time they decided to play Stack O' Pancakes, and Watson was almost suffocated under the other ones. Lips were blue and everything. You don't even need to give them a weapon. They'll always find a way."

Aubergine examined their little micro-society, as Wilson led a mini conga line, William on his heels, miming Wilson's marching band salutes. When Wendy tried to step out of the corner, William pointed his finger at her, a quiet scolding, and she stepped back into her spot. Watson barked, "Mush! Mush!" and Wendy yelled across the room, "Inside voice!" at the top of her lungs. At four, all on equal footing, a self-regulating force, Aubergine watched them all jockeying for leadership. It was all very fascinating.

"Why W? Why that letter?" Aubergine asked to no one in particular.

Bluebell passed it to Mark. He started carefully, "I know what sort of lifestyle these kids have. Beautiful home. Parents who love them and encourage them. We know they'll never have to worry about college money or what summer camp we can afford. That sort of adversity will always be," stopping to watch them play, "a myth to them. So," leaning on the counter and watching as Wendy escaped imprisonment and tackled Wilson at full speed, slamming him into the hardwood floor without mercy, "I guess I just wanted them to be picked last sometimes."

Aubergine nodded, and she was starting to understand Bluebell's stoic pride for her husband. "And I suppose you could only think of one or two names starting with a Z."

"Basically," he chuckled, grabbing a basting brush from a perfectly organized utensil rack and carrying on with his masterpiece.

The thought that went into this home. The focus and the attention they paid to parenting, to building patience, order, humility. Aubergine admired it on a level she didn't understand. Her life was a mish-mash of decisions that conflicted with one another.

The true love that consumed her... from the guy who hit her with a closed fist in a Taco Bell once.

The starvation diet that put her in the hospital... and the Best Dressed spread all in the same week.

The late night phone call to her high school best friend, just because she missed her... that resulted in a six month long feud.

The home she bought just to prove to Hollywood she wasn't "over" yet... that quietly foreclosed just a few months ago.

Unlike this home and this family, Aubergine lacked foresight all together.

She felt a tear fall before she could stealthily catch it. "I wish I had your brains," she said bashfully. She had their attention. "Sometimes I feel like," a songwriter, and yet she couldn't find the words. Aubergine swallowed and looked to her feet.

"Like a melody without a beat," Mark offered. She nodded humbly. "So find the beat, Aubergine. You're working backward. Start slow. Find the beat, and the song will build on top of it." The man had a way with words.

Aubergine ran a thumb under her eyes to correct any smudges. Bluebell pushed a hair from her sister's face and lovingly behind her ear. "You know what you need, little Sissy? You need some church."

All That Jazz

Now this was not a churchy family. Mother prayed to *a* god every chance she could. Bluebell distinctly remembered her baking a dish whose recipe she'd lost and watching as she leaned on the stove, shut her eyes, clasped her hands, and prayed, "Dear gods, please let this be the best chicken fried steak I've ever eaten," in all earnestness, the way one would pray for a cancer victim on his last lung. Thanking gods for breezy traffic, sunny days in December, free samples in the grocery store, this was her religion. The only day Mother dragged her family to an actual church was the Ascension Lutheran Arts and Crafts Bonanza, when they would travel the stables like troubadours, singing a cappella for tips. If it was a profitable day, Mother would say, "What a benevolent people, those holy rollers." The parishioners judged, so she judged back.

When Bluebell met Mark, however, it was on a Sunday. He was fresh out of church in a crisp white shirt and all the humility in his heart, and she was overcome with a radiant sort of light coming off of him. She decided from that day forward she was going wherever he was going.

Two weeks in the pews and Bluebell considered herself saved, begged for forgiveness for taking so long to hear the call, and erased curse words from her life's little sphere. Her dress neutralized, her hair morphed year by year into a solid and reliable armor. At that point she decided unconsciously that anything you needed to know about her would beam from her eyes and smile, and not the way her hips moved when she walked. It wasn't chastity, nothing self-righteous. She just wanted her own radiant light.

Somehow this Sunday Bluebell convinced Tim to attend. Maybe he was a little chagrined from bailing on their sleeping arrangements. Maybe it was because he had to show up at the house eventually if he had any plans of seeing his toothbrush or deodorant again, as hopping out of the Astro Van the day before was a pretty snap decision. When he walked in the door that morning, Mark greeted him with, "Just in time," and offered Tim a tie. He politely declined, but gave into peer pressure when the whole gaggle of smartly dressed Ws begged him to sit through church with them, strung up in their own decorative nooses. For that day anyway, he'd give in to being better dressed than Jesus.

"Come on, Uncle Tim, I'll teach you all the songs," Wendy said sweetly, her teeny tiny hand outstretched, ready to guide him up the steps into God's house. This felt just like one of those paintings with the cherub and the horn, he thought to himself. How do you say no to a four year old, especially one who is clairvoyantly tapped into his reluctance? Her eyes said *I know, man, I've been there*. But of course she hadn't. Wendy hadn't so much as been to daycare.

Mark stood at a pew and waved the hellions all into their spots, one kid for each adult hip as Bluebell slipped on her choir robe up front. She sat at the front of the church with a couple dozen other hymn enthusiasts, agog over this week's performance. On the end Wilson practically went missing, crammed tightly between the pew's wide end panel and Tim's comparatively monstrous shoulder. "Am I crushing you, kid?" Wilson shook his head. "You look like a snug bug in a rug," and the two grinned at each other.

Wilson opened his hymnal and looked at the illustrations in the margin designed to keep four year olds entertained. Wendy was on Tim's other side, thumb wrestling with Aubergine, who herself was getting a lot of stares from the locals. Either she didn't notice or was very good at tuning out audible gawks, or she was a very good actress, because all appearances were that she was perfectly comfortable with a wiggly toddler on either side of her, awaiting one killer sermon.

"Pay attention," Wilson whispered when he noticed Tim investigating the room casually for people he once knew. He slung an arm over the back of the pew and looked on to Wilson's hymnal. Eventually Pastor Mike was done greeting his troupe, spewed some madness about remorse and forgiveness, and finally the singing began.

Bluebell would never admit it aloud, but to her church was like a live music review. Like Broadway, the audience had to suffer through all the flamboyant dialogue to get to the good stuff, "All that jazz." The other choir members joked she should sing with a top hat and cane, her showmanship a hazard to anyone within rib-shot of her dancing elbows. If one positioned a hidden camera under Blue's robe, the world would be too distracted by her involuntary knee-knocking and shuffle stepping to notice what color underpants she was wearing. God could cover it with a robe, but that performer would always be in her.

Wilson, his mother's son, perked up at the sound of the conductor's stick tapping the ladies to attention.

As "Be Thou My Vision" began the room swayed, some stood and raised a couple hands over their heads, their chins up to the sky and eyes closed to the trusted care of the Lord. Wilson knew every word, even at four, and sang along as best he could despite not having any perspective on the words. "Riches I heed not, nor man's empty praise…" Tim considered there to be far too many S's in this song for any kid his age to execute without some major tongue cramping. "Thou mine inheriteth, now and alwayth…"

Tim felt a tap from Aubergine, and found her gesturing up to the front of the church, where Bluebell appeared to be rocking out. It wasn't uncommon for these choir singers to dance or incorporate some head bobbing for punctuation, but Bluebell was chock full of the spirit up there. "Thou and thou only, first in my heart," eyes shut, a fist clutching the robe against her chest, "High King of heaven, my treasure Thou art," both hands to the sky, looking to the ceiling as though Jesus himself was dangling from a support beam.

"Is she possessed?" Tim asked quietly.

"She looks like she's doing an impression of someone possessed."

Aubergine couldn't control the expression on her face. This was a ridiculous spectacle from where she was sitting. Maybe the others who were experiencing this Holy Ghost moment found Bluebell's style perfectly normal, perhaps admirable. But Auby wondered instead if her sister might have been drugged. She was so calm an hour ago, buttering toast and clicking the Ws into their seatbelts. Everything was routine, but this here, this was passion. Aubergine had no idea her sister was capable of passion. Earlier that day she witnessed Bluebell at what Auby thought was her maximum elation over a 20% off coupon for the kids' haircuts. She had no idea that was just a warm-up for Bluebell's small town brush with showbiz, and that she actually saved up all her week's worth of ardor just for hymns. The robes were so unflattering. Aubergine couldn't figure out the appeal.

Enough was enough and Tim couldn't hold it in any longer. He dropped his chin to his chest and did everything he could to muffle the sort of nasal laugh that sounds a lot like a semi truck throttling. This of course is contagious in a church, where all that devoted energy sits right at the surface waiting for the right trigger. First Aubergine, because her mind was already there, then the kids, one by one, crying their laughter right out of their eyes.

"What are we laughing at?" Wendy asked between giggles, not bothering to whisper. Neither had the heart to tell her how silly her sweet mother looked up there, but it didn't matter. Kids would much prefer a release like this to quiet reflection in church any day of the week and twice on Sunday. This Sunday, in fact.

Finally Mark gave them the signal with his chin and his converging eyebrows, suggesting maybe they take their disrespect outside. "I'm sorry," Aubergine mouthed, and the clowns scooted out the back door, feeling the scorn burn their backs the whole way out.

"Lose a ear, gain a year."

Outside the sun shone, a crisp but beautifully blue day. The kids couldn't tell the difference between 75 and 45 degrees at the rate they were scrambling around. Wendy as usual was asserting her dominance in any way she could being the only girl, executing choke holds, punching bread-baskets, using her patent leather shoe as a paddle. Aubergine slid on her Gucci shades and attempted to referee where she could, but motherhood wasn't one of her natural skills. She floundered at first, then realized it might be easier to let them go until one was crying. Just do what Blue does.

Tim looked on from a nearby car, where he was leaning with Wilson. "I'm sorry, kid, I gotta," he said, pulling out a pack of smokes.

"You shouldn't do cigarettes, Uncle Tim."

"I know, I know," he said, lighting one up. "I only smoke when I can't take it anymore," which was about hourly.

Wilson had no idea what that meant. He stuck his hands in his little pockets and watched his siblings let loose.

"So tell me about yourself, kid," Tim proposed, half interested.

"Well, my name is Wilson," *Wilthon*, "and I'm four and three quarter's years olds."

"Yeah, kid, I know that much. Tell me something I wouldn't already know if I talked to your mom about you."

Wilson considered this a second. "My favorite color is blue. Is that something you didn't know?"

Tim scoffed. "Come on, man. Blue? How obvious could you be?"

"I like blue," Wilson shrugged.

"Everyone says that, and everyone can't like blue. It's too easy. You gotta come up with a better answer than that. Blue says you're just like everybody else, and you can never, ever be like everybody else." He sucked in on his cig, "What's your second favorite?"

"I guess red?" Wilson asked.

"Okay. Red is now your favorite color. Most people don't have the balls to like red. Next topic: how about your hopes and dreams. Let's try that."

"I hope Christmas comes soon."

"Yeah, that's a good one. Christmas is fun for guys like you." Wilson nodded, having perhaps the deepest conversation of his life. "What do you want to be when you grow up?" Wilson shrugged. "Yeah, I guess it's a little early. I'll give you that. Tell me what your biggest fear is. What are you afraid of most in your life?" Wilson thought long and hard. "Spiders?" No reaction. "The dark?" Still nothing. "Boogie man? Famine? Nothing?"

"I guess I'm going to have to go with big dogs."

"Are you crazy? Dogs are sweet."

"Just big dogs. They're too mean."

"You don't know anything, kid. They aren't mean. Just because they're big doesn't necessarily indicate they're mean. You can't judge them just based on their size."

"But what if I think they're nice and then they try to eat me?"

Valid question coming from a child. If Tim tells Wilson not to judge a book by its cover, this kid could in fact be eaten by a giant dog. Wilson wasn't especially meaty, but to the right guard dog, he could make a nice light lunch. And then he'd never hear the end of it from Bluebell.

"Sometimes you just have to give dogs a chance. That doesn't mean you run up and kiss them, because you're right, you never know. You could trust some dog and the next thing you know, it eats your face." Wilson squinted up into the sun to look at him, wondering where this was going. "But you never know, one of those big old dogs could be your best friend one day."

"Yeah."

"And maybe that big dog is just afraid you're going to eat *him*, did you ever think of that?"

"I wouldn't do that!" Wilson vehemently objected.

"Hey, I know that. I can tell you're a good guy, but dogs don't speak human. To them you're practically a grizzly bear. They don't know you're cool." Wilson accepted that. "And whatever gave you the impression a dog would eat a kid like you anyway? Prejudice is dangerous, man. Someone you know get bit or something?"

"Yeah."

Whoops. "Oh."

"Raymond got his ear bit off."

"No shit? Who's Raymond?"

"He goes to my church."

Tim pointed with his cigarette, "This church?" Wilson nodded and rubbed his ear. "Did they ever sew his ear back on?" Wilson shook his head. "So there's some kid in there with no ears?"

Well, he's got one ear."

"Gross."

"Yeah."

Tim was bitten by a dachshund once in high school. He had a scar and some minor nerve damage in his hand, and still felt a little pain after long nights on the guitar. He thought better than to tell Wilson that though. He wanted this kid to hang onto whatever scraps of optimism he could, for as long as he could. "You be nice to Raymond, okay? The kid's probably going to have a rough time as it is. He doesn't need you picking on him on top of it."

"Yeah, I know. Dad says if you lose a ear, you gain a year," Wilson said, with his perfectly unsophisticated grammar. He crossed his arms and leaned against the car, watching his brothers and sister screw around as though he was above it. Tim believed young Wilson understood his dad's sentiment, and was impressed for that moment with the maturity it took to grasp the concept; that experience, negative or otherwise, fostered growth.

Then Tim's awe switched over to concern, concern that Wilson didn't want to be part of that little pack right now. He thought that maybe this kid, though the oldest of the Ws but still undeniably a four year old child, should just be exposed to rainbows and giggles, none of these adult revelations.

Instead Tim chose to spend a peaceful moment with his nephew. He finished his cigarette and listened to the faint chimes of the piano inside.

Above the Deli

While Frank was gone Lorraine had compiled a
colorful coterie of odd balls. It didn't appear any of them
were assholes, but he certainly faced a mountain of
judgment from them having returned from what they called
"not my war." Lorraine did what she could to diffuse their
preconceptions, expressed what a renaissance man he was,
that he could as easily rebuild a carburetor as he could
arrange a four-part harmony as he could tell you the names
of every state and city politician, their party affiliation, and
their voting record.

By contrast Roscoe and Floyd spit out propaganda
and hoped no one would test them on the details. They
played music by ear and hoped it was as appealing to others
as it was in their minds. (It generally was not.) And when
their cars broke down, they'd resigned their transportation
needs to "Moe and Joe," what they'd named their left and
right feet. Frank had every right to find Roscoe and Floyd
to be a couple of lazy liberals, but realized this was as
unfair as them calling him a baby killer, as so many
protestors had in his travels back to Milwaukee.

Lorraine was concerned about Frank settling into
this new world of theirs, about finding a place among the
free thinkers and Zen masters and poets and long hairs and
paisley prints that fluttered in and out of their home like
there was no door on the place. She'd accepted these
people as her family, seeing as how she had none other than
her new little unit with Frank and the baby. Her brothers
and sisters and earth mothers took care of her right back,
and so Frank knew there was no choosing. It was a package

deal. If he wanted Lorraine, he had to take the really bad poetry along with it.

He had his work cut out for him. Frank, the alpha male in every circle he'd ever run in, suddenly didn't have any power with these guys, not until he could show them what he could do musically.

One night Lorraine orchestrated it all perfectly. She said she and the baby were going to stay home and catch up on some sleep. Frank yawned along with her, said, "That sounds nice, I could use a nap."

"Actually I'm going to need you to drop that off at Roscoe's," she directed, pointing to a large casserole that looked cheesy and steamed at a too-dangerous-to-eat temperature.

"Why would I drop this off at Roscoe's when I can just eat this myself?"

Lorraine held the baby against her chest, her pink little face perfectly square with chub. Frank poked her cheek and made a popping noise, as though deflating a balloon. One day she'd find that as funny as he did, but for now she just stared at him, blank, like a baby does. "Because I promised him I'd bring something to their pot luck, and now I'm just too tired."

"I'm not tired, Lorrainey?" They were both parents to this adorable, screaming child, after all.

"Of course you are, but my tits are full of milk, not yours."

She walked right into it. "What tits?" Frank smiled, opting to indulge her this one night. He thought dropping off a dish, making fifteen minutes of forced pleasantries, and returning home to his family wasn't the worst lot in life, and would certainly reward him something down the line.

Roscoe and Floyd were roommates and lived in a piece of shit apartment on the North end of town, over a deli that may or may not have had mob ties to Chicago. The few times Frank had been there he thought for sure he was walking into an execution, but each time came away with a really good pastrami on rye, and so it was worth all the paranoia.

Walking up to their door he heard too many voices for his liking. The smell of pot crept under the door like a spirit entity in the hallway, and Frank felt an immediate regret. He wasn't too fond of parties. He didn't consider himself terribly social these days, particularly after he'd come home from overseas and realized he only related to an infant anymore. Even Lorraine was a bit too nutty to get her head around his recent experiences in Vietnam, so he mostly lived inside his thoughts, gave the world the mask that made them comfortable. It was easier than calling these people a bunch of worthless hippies and alienating himself from his wife.

"Frank!" Roscoe welcomed him, cigarette in hand, porkpie hat sitting high over his eyes. Frank entered with his signature limp, which no one ever dared acknowledge, and gave a withholding wave to the ten or fifteen beatniks who'd gathered. "Where's our girl?"

"With the baby, but she didn't want to leave you high and dry," he passed the casserole to Roscoe. "I hope it hasn't gotten cold."

"Well, that's real nice of you to come out all this way," Roscoe said sincerely, and placed the dish on a table along with a few other plates that didn't look half as good or required as much effort. A plate with carrot sticks, store-bought dip, a platter with five or six unsliced blocks of cheese, a baguette, and wine. Lots of red wine. "Hey, everyone, this is Frank, Lorraine's wife- err, husband. Sorry about that, man."

"It's fine," he replied, not loving this moment. Every eye was on him. Frank hated parties. He clearly didn't fit in with this crowd. His hair like an oil-slick and his shirt tucked in neatly, he didn't see his kind anywhere. This was Lorraine's world, he knew that. He'd experienced enough of her crazy talk to know what kind of company she'd been keeping. He'd heard her say in their company:

> "Do you think history majors are reincarnated? By studying the past, they probably feel a closer connection to their former selves."

Or,

> "I love red headed children, but I don't trust them."

Or,

> "How many hands do you think touched this food before it got to us? I can just feel the intimacy on my tongue when I eat it."

And these people got her, and loved her.

"Hey, man, you play drums?" Floyd asked him, without saying hello first.

"I can."

"You any good?"

"I'm okay. I can play everything a little bit, but I'm not great at any one instrument, per se." Frank tried to keep his voice low, not wanting attention. Not for that.

"So you play more than just drums?"

"Horns, guitar, piano, whatever."

Floyd couldn't believe his fortune. "You some kind of genius?"

"No, I just dabble here and there." This exposure was making him sweat. He hated parties. "I write a little."

"You write music, and you're just now telling us this?" Roscoe exclaimed. Frank shuddered at the waft of air he felt when every head turned to size him up now that was claiming to be a musical savant, apparently. He knew damn well that no one believes you're a musician until you're successful at it. A writer is a bartender, until he's a published author. A guitarist is a machinist, until he's playing his own music somewhere live. A painter has a cute hobby, until some New York snob discovers his genius.

Until an artist is "discovered," people roll their eyes over their pastime, pity the time spent toiling at an unrequited dream. For that reason he didn't dream at all. He frittered in his solitude, strummed over Lorraine's hums, and sometimes he didn't realize it, but he would tap rhythms with his heels and toes during dinner. Lorraine noticed, at first thinking it was a nervous tick, but then realized just about any time his mind was idle, his feet were working an invisible drum kit. And that's where her plan to pair him with these two fruit loops on a bad end of town was born. She knew Frank needed this if he was going to ever get back into this world again.

"I'm not very good," Frank bullshitted.

"Lorraine said you knew beats, and we're looking for a drummer. Basically we need a lot of work. You want to jam a little? See if we got chemistry?"

Floyd's little musical mating ritual was giving Frank the heebie jeebies. Men don't talk like this. Or they shouldn't. He *hated* parties.

"Come on, man. I'll make you some cheese and whatever it was you brought over. We'll drink some wine, see what gels." Roscoe's approach was a little easier to digest, even with that lame Hawaiian shirt he was wearing.

The night wore on, and by the end of it Frank was in a band. They were awful, but he brought structure to their little hodge-podge, pointed out a better tempo for a too-slow song, brought intensity to another song that previously read like carousel music. This band needed him.

This band also needed a name, and they spent the better part of the next week shooting ideas over the phone. No hello, no intro, just Frank picking up the phone and Roscoe saying calmly, "Ruthless Drifter," and then Frank would hang up politely, his silence representing his vote. "Cat Calls." "The Black Beans." "The Mice." "Merciless Love." All rejected.

On the ride home that night Frank came back to himself a bit. Being with Roscoe and Floyd, some weed, and all their collaboration, all their need for his insights, it generated something new in him, like the singularity for some new element all together. This kind of power brewed in his gut like a new star, rotating and heating up and spewing sparks of energy out from his center to his fingers and toes and eyeballs. Red lights were redder, wet streets were shinier, the thunk-thunk of his feel up the stairs a little more baritone.

He couldn't wait to open up that door, knowing his sweetheart was on the other side, knowing that if the world looked the way it did all of a sudden, certainly she'd be a heightened version of Lorraine. Not a Lorraine, but a LORRAINE! A little curlier, a little raspier, her skin a little frecklier. He couldn't contain it, who cared if it woke the baby. He charged through the door like it was his first breath swimming up from the bottom of the ocean. Open it went, slamming against the wall behind it, except when he saw her, expecting to see a brighter smile, a rounder shoulder, a glow coming off of her like a lighthouse beam, it wasn't at all like he could have envisioned.

It was better.

Crotch-Shots

After church Tim rescued Aubergine from the confines of domesticity and took her somewhere more comfortable: Mutt's Bar and Grill. Sure it was a shithole, but it was small and dark and the Gladney legacy couldn't fit in the front door.

Tim was 26 and Aubergine was 28, both far too young to be cooped up in a house dominated by bed-wetters. At Mutt's however, they were easily the youngest people in the joint. Aubergine leaned on the palm of her hand and examined her fellow Sunday day drinkers. All a little too heavy, making noises from the backs of their throats to clear their phlegm passages, eyes glued to a muted SportsCenter, the tails of their polo shirts exposing the cracks of their asses for all the world to admire. "Where are the wives, pray tell?" she asked to nobody. Someone should have checked these men before they left the house.

Nobody stared at Tim, so he was more than happy to sit and ferment among the cavemen.

"Why do you think Bluebell has such a hard time with Mother and Father?" Aubergine wondered aloud, examining her pretzel for an approximate calorie count.

"Sounds like you're the one having the hard time."

"Au contraire, mon frère. Bluebell is blocking. My life coach told me all about this at Promises," she began to preach, hand to her heart and eyes closed.

"Oh, Jesus, here we go."

"Bluebell is suppressing anger. It's so obvious. She is as pissed off as any of us. It's written all over her. She thinks if she keeps busy being some perfect robot daughter they'll finally love her."

"You're ruining a perfectly good song, Auby." The jukebox spun Johnny Cash religiously, and at this moment "It Ain't Me, Babe" crawled the walls in that signature slow burn. That man knew how to set a mood.

"What good does that do, you know? One day she's just going to have a fucking moment, you know? She's going to be in the grocery store and some old lady is going to be spanking her kids or something, and Bluebell is just going to flip the fuck out, and then she's going to realize after all this time that her Mother is completely evil. Evil!" She waited for Tim's response, who was staring ahead at a Sunday morning football analysis. "You know?"

"*You know*?" mocking her in what is famously known as every grade school kid's mongoloid voice. "Auby, saying 'you know' over and over again, it's obnoxious. How badly do you need my reassurance?"

"What's that supposed to mean?"

"You know?" Tim snapped back.

Aubergine leaned back in her barstool, flustered. "What the fuck is your problem, Timothy?"

He considered for a second how wise it was to have this particular conversation in what he called his happy place, with a beer already down the hatch. "Has it ever occurred to you that you both are doing what you need to do to get by in all this? Yeah, she's fruit loops. She's doing everything she can to reincarnate Donna Reed. She's the anti-Lorraine. But clearly that works for her. So what if she's got something to prove to Mother. Blue is happy. Crazy, sure, but happy."

Flabbergasted, Auby choked back disgust. "Uh, ex-ca-use me, that is bullshit. She is not happy."

"And you are? You are the archetypical Daddy-issues pop star."

"WHAT?" like a verbal missile. Aubergine was pissed.

Tim rattled the evidence off, finger by finger, never taking his eyes off the TV. "Rebellious youth. Leaving home for Hollywood. Hungry for acceptance from your adoring fans. Rehab. Paparazzi crotch-shots. Going out with scumbags. Come on, Aubs. It's like you're following a manual or something. If you didn't have any musical ability you'd be a stripper."

Aubergine sipped her cocktail carefully, ignoring him. "Do you know how long it's been since I've had one of these? No one in L.A. can make a decent Brandy Old Fashioned. They use one of those premixed things. It's an insult."

"And you have to consider that she had different parents than you and me."

"Yeah, why is that? How come when they had her they were normal? What was so wrong with us that they had to completely lose their shit?"

Tim signaled the bartender for another beer. "They were never normal. I think they just got along back then. Before us, they still loved each other, so they loved

Bluebell. But when we came, they hated each other, so they hated us."

Aubergine hurt for him, wondering when he came to this revelation on his own. What night of drinking ended with this as a satisfactory explanation? "You think so?"

For Tim it was a matter of fact. He'd accepted it. "Am I wrong about it? I mean, it is what it is."

"You really think they hated us?" She prayed for a different truth.

Tim shoveled a handful of pretzels in his mouth and decided, "Yeah." It was what it was.

The music turned over a few times, Hank Williams, Loretta Lynn. The siblings reconnected as they always had before, gravitating back to their comfort zone of anything but the torment of their youth.

> "You've got a tattoo of a TransAm on your neck, and you're making fun of my crotch-shots?"

And,

> "What's the lowest amount of money someone would need to pay you to move back to Milwaukee? A million? Five?"

And,

> "Which one is Watson and which one is William? Are any of them Weston?"

And potential song lyrics on the backs of Mutt's cocktail napkins, harmonizing to LeAnn Womack, strangers holding their lighters in the air off in the shadows, "I bet you're in a baaar, listenin' to cheatin' song...," remembering the last time he house-sat for her while she was on tour and he got a taste of L.A. success. They recounted the good times like confirmation it had all really happened. And recounted the bad times as though they were signing a pact to never leave the other one behind, to always be there for one another when the world let them go. They were all each other had.

The Ghost

"**Brookfield** High School, Home of the Bobcats." The foreboding sign greeted her over the door like the ninth gate of hell.

Aubergine's years at BHS weren't the worst in the world, to be fair. She wasn't the pretty girl who grew up nerdy and bespectacled. She pretty much exited the womb shapely and tan. The boys loved her no matter how poorly she treated them, the girls wanted her to die in a tragic teen drunk driving accident, closed casket preferably. She was nice, but that only mattered so much when she was the girl standing between that guy and every other girl.

Being at her old high school on a Sunday was kind of like of a stroll through a haunted house. The trophy case still displayed all her life's early triumphs, despite this generation not giving half a damn about any of it. Students passing it didn't care about the 1988 Girls' Lacrosse Achievement. *Time to melt that trophy down already*, Aubergine thought to herself. A team photo of this year's celebrated football team sat center stage, all the haircuts looking progressive even for her taste, as though part of a uniform. She remembered this sort of lock-step, herself leading the trend of red lipstick in her day.

At the lower corner of the case she saw her very own contribution to Brookfield's storied legacy. A humble trophy shoved into the corner like that old grandmother whose voice has gone too frail to be heard. "State Choral Champion," it read simply. No photo, no names listed. Not a big budget set aside for singing champs. Aubergine realized with a sigh that in this haunted house *she* was the ghost, and that gave her the chills. She was rattling chains and slamming doors without anyone caring where it was coming from.

The halls echoed with her every step. The floors had been replaced since her time there, she could see her blurry reflection in them. Those halls didn't see stilettos very often, and the click-click bounced off the lockers in perfect time, like a metronome.

Aubergine pushed her nose up against the glass of her old science lab. Mr. Morello was right out of college and was the subject of much speculation. Auby could spot a gay guy a mile away even back then. To protect his reputation, she helped perpetuate a rumor about him having an affair with a married woman. It made sense at the time. A few doors down, Creative Writing with Mrs. Chevalier, the room to this day still decorated with tapestries and medieval masks. The woman was batty, but she could turn hormonal surges into creative juices. She was one of Aubergine's miracle workers in the early years.

All these legends from her youth, still existing where she remembered them, as though Auby never had.

She got a little turned around but eventually found her old music room. It was in this very space her jazz band took shape, her temporary hip-hop trio was born, and she and her brother wrote and performed countless folk harmonies. The room was tiered to accommodate the school orchestra. Aubergine walked up the levels backward, remembering how it felt to be in that room so many years ago, like intruding on her own past. She stood in her favorite spot from so many years before, up at the top by the big window. The dust travelled the room and glittered in the beam of sunshine shooting in from behind her.

"Are you an angel or just a burglar?" a man's voice asked her. She stood in silhouette, and he thought for sure there was no way it was really her.

Aubergine stepped out from the beam to see it was Mr. Leeney, the very same music director that ran the room in her era. She doubted he'd remember her. "Sorry, I'm an old student. Just in town. Visiting. Thought I'd take a look around."

Mr. Leeney shielded his eyes and squinted at her, "Aubergine Gladney?" She smiled, gave a small wave. "Well, I'll be."

"Hi, Mr. Leeney." He looked great, trim as ever. The same khakis and light blue button-down she remembered, 34 inch waist to this day, broad shoulders. "Here on a Sunday?"

"There's always more to do. No interruptions on a Sunday. Are you visiting your family? I heard about your dad. I'm so sorry."

"Yeah, thanks. The funeral's in a few days."

"Of course." He didn't quite know what to say to her about it. There's never a right thing.

She edged down a couple steps, "I'm sorry to bother you. I'll get out of your hair. It's just been so long since I've been home. Guess I was feeling a little nostalgic."

Mr. Leeney waved that off, "Don't be silly. Have a seat. It's an honor to have you back here. One of my success stories." Aubergine took a seat at the piano beach, he at his desk. "How does it feel to be back?"

"Weird."

"I'll bet. Home feels less like home every time you come back." Mr. Leeney had to be in his 40's at this point, but he still had that easy relatability the kids loved so much way back when. A little more salt and pepper, but basically the same guy, the same ease to him. He was the only teacher that cared more about her development musically than the length of her skirts.

"How's Mrs. Leeney?" Aubergine's arch nemesis, Vice Principal Leeney, took it upon herself to be Auby's mother when her own stopped showing up to things, but in the worst way.

Mr. Leeney shifted in his seat, crossed his arms. "She's good. Remarried by now."

Aubergine shirked, "I didn't even know you'd divorced.

He nodded, uncomfortable. "About," he counted backward, "well I suppose it was a year or so after you left town."

"I'm sorry," she said softly. He shrugged. "Sounds like I was the glue keeping you together," she joked. He laughed.

"Turned out for the best. Things always do." *Do they? Always?* she wondered. Aubergine hated the concept of "everything happens for a reason," because most of her life's travails had largely ended up purposeless. Her life was a cycle of misfortune, hunger, and survival. Nowhere in that cycle was there epiphany or victory or any sort of conclusion. Just a wheel rolling uncontrollably down a rocky hill. When she made it to Promises and the admissions coordinator interviewed her, she asked "Do you feel you've hit your bottom?" Aubergine's answer was, "There is no bottom."

They sat there quietly for a second, absorbing each other's energy. "Looks like the school got a nose job."

Mr. Leeney thought about it, took a gander around. "We all did," he said cheerfully, in no way referring to her obviously ill-fitting breasts. "You look fantastic! The last time I saw you your hair was experimental."

Aubergine laughed, "That's being kind." She pushed a lock behind her ear. "So what do I call you now? I'm over 18 now, you know."

"Gerard. Please call me Gerard."

Ah, yes. Gerard. She's forgotten he was a real person with a real first name. She evaluated that. "I don't think I can. Feels too weird."

"Too bad."

"Can't I call you Sir instead?"

"Only if you want me calling you Ma'am."

"Well, that's not going to happen," she balked. "But *Gerard*? I don't know about this."

"If you call me Mr. Leeney, I'm calling you Ms. Gladney. Although I'd bet that might be welcome relief for you. Being Aubergine, I bet your checks don't even read your last name."

"I wish that was true," it was true. "Okay, so Gerard it is. Gerard. Gerard. Gotta practice that one. Gerard. That's one of those names that starts to sound like a made up word the more you say it. Gerard. Am I saying it right? I think I abused it." Her voice trailed off. She tapped on a piano key so softly it barely sounded. "Can I ask you something, Gerard?"

"Please."

She felt the need to guard herself, years of Hollywood had bruised her. "Can we have some sort of teacher-student confidentiality?"

"I solemnly swear," he held up his right hand.

Aubergine waited. This was a toughy. She cleared her throat, and when she finally spoke her voice still had one of those bubbles blocking her windpipe, making her question even more awkward and uncomfortable than she'd anticipated. "What do you think of me?" She swallowed, tried to maintain eye contact.

"In what regard?"

"What I mean is, am I…a…joke to you?"

Gerard leaned back in his seat. "Well, this is interesting. I don't think you'd be asking me that if you didn't already feel that way about yourself."

"Jeez, Mr. Leeney. If I wanted psycho-babble I'd go back to fake-rehab," she joked. But he didn't laugh.

"Are people treating you like you're a joke, Aubergine?" She cocked her head, *maybe*. "I don't think anything about your life is funny. I think- may I be frank?" She nodded. "All I know about you is a combination of magazine covers and a memory of a talented young teenager with fame in her eyes. So maybe this isn't fair of me to say, but I'd actually consider your life a little tragic."

She was overcome with this moment, her eyes welled, and she wiped her tear before it could fall. A communiqué directly to her soul she couldn't even prepare a canned reaction for.

Gerard continued. "You had it all. Or people thought you did. And they all said you were careless with your career. I disagree. I think you're very much the same girl who used to sit up in that seat and stare out the window," he gestured up the steps. "You're still looking. You haven't even found your career yet."

"What's so tragic about that? According to you my life is just beginning."

Gerard planned his words carefully, then leaned forward and looked right through her eyes and into her brain, close enough she couldn't look away if she tried. "The tragedy is that no matter what happens for you, you're always going to live in your past. When I see you in the headlines, I just think to myself how unhappy you must be. And that's not because of your circumstances. It's because no matter how far away you get from Wisconsin, you're still right back here. You won't really let yourself leave."

Aubergine was offended. "I just think it's important never to forget where you came from." She'd used this sound bite on every talk show, knowing full well it was horse shit.

"Aubergine, if I can give you any advice, and this is just coming from Gerard Leeney, high school music teacher, it's that you absolutely forget where you came from. Erase it completely."

"You think I'm living in the past."

"I think you're drowning in it, Aubergine."

"You can tell all that from a couple of tabloids?"

"The whole world can. Every person standing in every supermarket checkout line is wondering how old you're going to be when you die. And I don't mean from natural causes."

She gasped. "Jesus Christ, Mr. Leeney."

"I know it's harsh. But you look lost. And lost people don't exactly build schools for poor kids in Africa. They self destruct."

He was right. She damn well knew it.

Maybe he had affection for her enough not to think of her as a joke, but the rest of the world didn't know her when she was an innocent just wanting to write songs. They knew the gossip rags, which mostly weren't just gossip. And they were all standing by, waiting for an overdose. The irony of ironies was that any implication of drug abuse was leaked by her publicists, and she hadn't so much as smoked pot in years. In all actuality, she didn't need drugs to sink into herself, but being naturally implosive didn't sell records. Eventually the public gives up on the spoiled and the angry.

Aubergine felt a wave of panic inching its way up from her stomach to her throat to the back of her mouth, drying up her tongue in an instant. She had to excuse herself on account of her own discomfort, and despite his apologies and sympathies, she had to get out of there.

Turning the corner into the hallways she let her tears go. Years of fear and self-hate culminating into a rush of grunts and sobs she couldn't control. "Erase it completely," she repeated to herself as she raced through the maze of halls.

"Where's the goddamn exit?" she hollered. Maybe she was losing her mind, maybe she'd been gone too long, but she couldn't find her way out of the school. She had this nightmare every night of her life, being stuck in a building, having every intention of doing great things once outside, but never being able to get out of there. Usually it was her childhood home, and she was trapped upstairs, contemplating a leap from her bedroom window just to escape it at any cost. Every time it came to that, the window wouldn't open.

Finally she happened upon her old locker, her initials still etched into it, a lifetime branding. She said to herself the day she did it, graduation day, that she'd never be back, and that there needed to be evidence in the world she existed there once. This was always her compulsion. In just about every pocket of the country and many in Europe, she'd sunk her hand into some wet concrete, carved her name into an old closet door, hid personal treasures in the sand. Once she wrote a note on the back of a receipt and slipped it into the pocket of a teenager she sat across from in a Parisian café. The forlorn kid sat alone in silence and ignored the book he'd brought with him, opting to stare into his coffee cup and dream away in his thoughts. Her note read, "You're not alone," and afterward she wished she'd taken the time to figure out how to write that in French instead.

Here she was years later and those initials were quelling a panic attack. She closed her eyes and ran her fingers over the letters, reading them like Braille. She slid her hand down the door to the latch and tried to open it, but it was locked. The only logical thing to do was to smash her fist into it as hard as her spindly little arms could muster. She felt the shock of that solid surface shoot up her arm and stun her shoulder.

"Hey!" A security guard just barely of college age caught her mid-fury and raced over to assess the situation.

"Sorry, my fault!" she whimpered, trying to sound calm, and jammed her shades on her face as quickly as she could, race walking in the opposite direction. "My mistake, it's cool," she waved over her shoulder, hoping he wouldn't recognize her.

The guard's hand came down upon her shoulder hard, and yanked her back at a force that to her seemed disproportionate to the offense. "Miss, that is school property." Like he gave a shit.

Aubergine did everything she could to conceal her face. Flashbacks of the paparazzi catching her slapping that tattoo artist across the face came to mind, and the subsequent shame. "I know, I'm so sorry. It's my mistake, I'm leaving now."

"Not a chance." He dialed 911 into his fancy phone. Aubergine decided not to resist for the time being, then take off running as soon as he trusted her. Kind of a reverse Stockholm Syndrome. She wondered how quickly that took effect. "No shit," the guard realized finally, "you're Aubergine!"

"No, I'm just, uh, we're cousins. People make that mistake all the time."

"Whatever. It's totally you. You're her." He switched his phone to camera mode and set its focus on her.

"What the hell would Aubergine be doing in Wisconsin? That's ridiculous." He wasn't convinced, just grinned into his phone's display. "I'm Fa...Faronda."

Zooming right in on her face, "That's the lamest fake name I've ever heard. Oh, man, my friends aren't going to believe this. Hang on," he paused, attempting to attach a subject line of "ABRJEAN! FCKN A!" to the photo he sent to his entire contacts list.

Just then, acting on impulse, Aubergine grabbed the phone and smashed it into the kid's forehead, hard enough that bits of technology flew in every direction, including inward so that they were embedded in the kid's scalp. "OW! MOTHER! FUCKER!" he yelled at her, appalled, tapping his head with his fingers and looking at them for blood. Realizing what she'd done, Aubergine made a run for it, and of course now that she, a recognizable face, had broken so many laws, this was when the exit happened to appear right around the very next corner.

Behind her she heard the wailing coming from the poor kid, who she knew was fine, but she knew would also describe the incident as a "when celebrities attack" sort of moment, and recount the details with heavy embellishment to everyone he could. Possibly a lawyer. With haste Aubergine raced straight to the double doors leading to her freedom from this mistake of a day and *ka-chug*, the door flew open and the rush of November hit her face like a cold reality.

The reality of the police officers that had just parked and were radioing for back-up.

Plastics

Eventually Lorraine needed Frank to get serious. The band was a great weekend treat. She loved having her best friends at the apartment so many nights, creating, creating, creating, but the apartment wasn't paying for itself. Coming home to a menagerie of musicians and their instruments was little respite from her job waiting tables, one kaleidoscope of noise replaced with another. At one point she was somewhere in that mix, an integral contributor to their creations. Now she just made sandwiches and rocked the baby. Time certainly kept moving, like the flow of people through her home, regardless of Lorraine's evolving role.

Luckily they'd struck a convenient little arrangement with the Swingin' Door off Michigan Street. The band would play Saturday nights until they couldn't fill the room anymore, and Frank would work whatever muscle the bar needed for just about every other night of the week. The pay was obscenely low enough he didn't worry about another band coming in and taking their spot, knowing well enough no one else was that crazy.

Nights at the bar, days with his Bluebell, and whatever hours he could eek out with Lorraine. It was a hectic schedule, this real life of his, but to him it was ideal. They had no savings, no plan whatsoever. They just woke and figured it out as it came, and to him that was all the adventure he needed.

The flipside of the coin of course was Lorraine, whose day shifts at the Silver Dollar Diner slowly squeezed her dry of any girlish enthusiasm she had left. She was the best thing that ever happened to that greasy spoon, she knew it, the customers knew it. Milwaukee was a pair of rams steaming at the nose- angry long haireds on one end, the Catholic collegiate on the other. But Lorraine was her own breed, smarter than those other girls, smarter than most guys even, more grounded than her flower-power cohorts, all with the limitless vision that led Frank to believe miracles got them where they were, and they would come on the regular, like the seasons.

But with the seasons, more and more she reminded herself of what her efforts, her encouragement, her pep talks, her courage and her sacrifice had gotten them, and convinced herself he was less a provider and more a beneficiary. The resentment started with just one cell, like a cancer, and her bones ached a little more every damn day, just enough not to notice it, until it completely got away from her control.

Once a week their neighbor would watch Bluebell so that Lorraine could put on something sheer and effervescent and be Frank's proudest achievement, next to the band of course, and Bluebell, and his military past, which he hung onto even when it was unpopular to. She was somewhere in that stew, which would have been fine in the early days. So, Saturdays being the prettiest girl in the room mattered more to her than he knew.

Roscoe's bright idea for a name, "Daylight Dreamer," didn't pack the punch Frank was looking for (his vote was for "Ghost Ship"), but it caught on and a bevy of under aged nymphs assembled at the foot of the stage every week. Of course Frank noticed. The stage was his little metaphor for a lifetime of women lining up to meet him,

before there was a band, before there was Lorraine, before
the Army. But he didn't care about those girls. It was
flattering, but whenever a girl got too close after a set, he
had a bird call for either Roscoe or Floyd, whomever he
thought would be interested, to swoop in and take the run-
off for him. Frank had all he needed at home, with the only
girls who could ever hold his attention. It wasn't even a
struggle.

Try telling that to Lorraine. She kept her
insecurities hidden, but only so much, and Frank did what
he could to remind her of that first week in bed when they
forgot to eat. They woke up on day three and realized those
pains in their stomachs needed to be subdued, and not just
suffocated with more sex. "Gotta refuel the rocket ship," he
told her then, and still used to this day, usually with a sweet
wink for her, their secret little history under those blankets.

She did what she could to accept this path, but
whataboutmes crept into her thoughts every so often. When
Daylight Dreamer's local hit was given a spin on the radio
station, the disc jockey howling over the clever lyrics and
riffs, *What about me?*, she asked the car radio. After all,
she'd written the chorus and the second verse, as an
afterthought, just an aside while assembling lunch for the
boys. And when the neighbor knocked on the door just to
compliment him on his vocal range, she could hear him
singing in the shower through her pipes, Lorraine said *What
about me?* to her soul. She was always the better singer of
the two, and frequently let it rip in the shower herself.
Where was the neighbor after all those goosebump
inducing Aretha Franklin numbers?

"Baby?" she sidled to him one night, the rare ten
minutes they had together in the apartment that week. She
had been washing dishes. He was on the couch with
Bluebell, his little blooming flower, who was sleeping in a

perfect mold to his left side. Frank was awake, but only just barely. The night before was a late one. "Frank?"

"Shhh," he smiled.

Lorraine sat softly on the arm of the couch, slinging a kitchen towel over her shoulder. The picture was too precious to disturb. She spoke in a whisper. "So I was talking to the Koch's. Downstairs? Remember them?"

"Is she the one with the mustache?"

"You're terrible. But yes."

"How are the Koch's, baby?"

"They're great actually. They just bought a house." Her voice rose a bit on the *house* part.

Frank felt a pang of ineptitude, he wasn't sure why. She hadn't accused him of falling short yet. Not explicitly. "That's great. How can they afford that?"

"I didn't tell you? He's been working out at that plastics plant in Waukesha. It only took them a year to save for their down payment. I guess they're all union over there, so the pay is pretty good."

Like a big juicy turkey smothered in duck fat, he could smell a scheme sweating from her pores. Lorraine's eyes pled for him to take the bait without her having to go so far as to say the words aloud. He wasn't giving it to her. He lay there silent, clutching their little Bluebell, now three, with one giant paw.

"Just think. Bluebell could have her own room." Currently she was sleeping right in between them most nights, occasionally on the pull-out couch they'd "inherited" when a neighbor was evicted. "A yard. A kitchen that you can't see from the bed." These were legitimate desires. Where they were truly rooted, Frank had his doubts of their purity.

"I want those things, too, Lorrainey. But there's no way I can afford that. We do okay with the bills we have. Let's not push it."

"I'm glad you asked." He hadn't. "As it turns out there's an opening at the plant. It's at the bottom rung-"

"You know I can't work days, baby."

Lorraine had to consider her hand here. She could allow a bit of her depression to untangle itself little by little in front of him, give just a little more attitude every day, a few more despondent glances till she got what she wanted. She could drag it out until finally he took responsibility for her tumble into despair, and then give in, as he always did. But there wasn't time for that. The position at the plant would go quickly.

"I just," the puppy eyes, fingernails picking nervously at each other, "I guess I see all these other mothers we know, working hard, making sacrifices for their husbands and their children. And they are all getting houses in the suburbs. They're all getting new cars. And I ask myself, what about me? When will that time come for me?" A faux exhausted sigh, and the scheme was less juicy turkey and more a bald, raw bird, slapped down in front of him, guts and bits splattered in his general direction. He saw it coming, and still had no power to thwart it.

So this was how it was going to be, he thought to himself. Lorraine could play this card for the rest of her life, hold the burden of replacing her dreams with his like the scales of justice. It's not as though the thought had escaped him. He'd just hoped she'd given up her life on stage willingly, that being a mother was enough for Lorraine. But he was wrong, and most nights while he was at the Swingin' Door, she stared out a window and remembered. Her music, the feel of the lights on her face and the bass under her feet. If she couldn't have it, neither should he.

If you asked him, he loved their life. He didn't mind opening his eyes and seeing his entire apartment without having so much as to crane his neck. He didn't mind making just enough. Just enough money equaled time with his family, the opportunity to make music and share camaraderie with these guys, a feeling he hadn't experienced since boot camp. But any man, even with the world in the palm of his hand, doubts he's living the best way. It's their nature. It's how their fathers ruin them.

The reality was he had a score to settle with Lorraine, and he owed her this one thing. Still, the vision of himself in a plastics plant, it felt like death.

Frank reached out to her with his foot, rubbing her thigh with his socks, Bluebell all heavy breaths and dream twitches. "I'm going to need a tie, right?"

Lorraine grinned, the creases of her outer eyes folding together like their own little smiles. Frank loved that bashful look on her, like she didn't believe she deserved his generosity, which of course they both knew was a lie. She pulled the strings, however good she was at giving him the illusion of control. But this look, this rush of blood to her cheeks, he was a sucker for it. He didn't see that on her often.

"I think there are a few in a box somewhere."

Frank wondered if Bluebell could feel, through osmosis, through the emissions travelling from his head out to his limbs and over to her little frame, that this was when everything changed. He wondered if in her dream that sunny day on the beach with puppies dancing around her, that the water suddenly went choppy and a thunderstorm loomed and the puppies stared out at the sea with their tails between their legs. Did her dreams feel the shift?

Silver Platter

A night in jail isn't a big deal for someone like Aubergine. Not that she loved it, because it was less than pleasant no matter what city she was in. Las Vegas jail wasn't a luxury hotel, and Beverly Hills jail was no Beverly Hills. Luckily this was Waukesha County Jail, and other than a couple shoplifters and a barely-18 graffiti artist, she basically had the joint to herself. She'd been in much worse conditions before.

A night in jail is a big deal to someone like Bluebell, whether or not she was the one doing the time. In this case she imprisoned herself in the Astro Van and begged that Mark be the one to bail her sister out, fill out the paperwork, face the scrutiny. He's Mark, Wonder Husband, so he obliged.

The process took about an hour, and eventually Aubergine emerged from the fluorescent lit cinderblock hallway. It was 11:30 at night, and by then her church clothes had been wrinkled and marred by random strains. A skid of grass on her knee, Old Fashioned remnants on her collar, chalk on her elbow, security guard blood on her boob.

"Smells in there," she said, hugging Mark weakly. "And I'm starving."

He waved at the officer who processed her, and escorted her out the front door with a hand on the small of her back. "You okay?"

"Mmmhmm," she answered. "Where's Bluebell?"

"In the car. She's not happy. Just a warning."

"Well," she sighed, "I wasn't expecting a sympathy card."

They walked briskly through the parking lot and up to the van, where Bluebell was polishing off a family sized bag of Doritos. She was a stress eater. Upon seeing them she hopped out of the passenger seat and tortilla chip shards sprinkled from her clothes like confetti. "I don't even know what to say to you," she hissed. Her hands were bright orange.

"I know, Sissy."

Bluebell opened Aubergine's door, then buckled her in like a child. She looked her sister in the face, making sure she had Auby's full attention. "Jail?" She took a breath. "*Jail?*" Aubergine didn't answer, so Bluebell got back in the passenger seat and the van puttered along out of the lot. "I'm not sure you know how embarrassing it is to have Mr. Leeney call you and say the words, 'Your sister was arrested for vandalism, assault, and evading arrest.'"

"I didn't evade arrest. It just looked that way because I was running."

"I expect this from Tim. But not you, Aubergine. Not you."

Auby spaced out, numbed herself to what little nighttime scenery she could make out through the window tint.

Bluebell turned around in her seat to face her sister, who looked pale and small in her little space. "When I knew you both were coming I said to Mark, 'It will be good

to have Sissy here so we can talk some sense into Tim.'
Didn't I, Mark?" Mark nodded, spun the wheel around.

"Tim doesn't need your sense, Bluebell."

"Don't bother with your big house wisdom,
Malcolm X." Blue pointed a "cheese" covered finger at her
sister. "Don't you know that mug shot is going to be
everywhere in the morning?" Auby's stomach flipped. She
had forgotten about the mug shot. Always with the mug
shot. "It's like you're handing Mother insults on a silver
platter. She didn't have anything recent to draw from, but
thank you very much, now she's going to have no problem
coming up with some fresh material. Aubergine, why do
you do this to yourself? Why do you make it so easy for
everybody?" As though it all was a conscious decision on
her sister's part.

Auby didn't answer. Her sister was right to ask, and
there was no logical answer at this time. She just didn't
know any other way to live.

"Can we just find a McDonald's that's still open?"

Mark smiled at her in the rearview, her blip of
solace, before Bluebell gave up on her and faced front in a
huff.

Smoke

Monday morning was like any other for Bluebell. The only difference this particular day was that while her husband spread preserves on toast and Blue hustled to get the kids dressed before it was embarrassingly late to be seen in their pajamas by neighboring stay-at-homes, her sister's snores billowed down the stairs like a wafting fart. "That girl can blow," Mark chuckled.

"How cute are the kids today?" Bluebell cooed. "Every so often they have a really cute day. I don't know where it comes from, but I love it." She had a way. Bluebell could shove out whatever she wanted simply by making the choice. She shoved out the confusion of how her parents treated her siblings, she shoved out the fact that Mark's career was nurtured and hers was obliterated, she shoved out Tim abandoning the family, she shoved out Aubergine's most recent night in jail, and all the previous nights for that matter. She could shove it all out and decide today was a beautiful day and she would prove it by what she wore (pink) and how she beamed (brilliantly).

William was brushing Wendy's hair with all the focus of a professional. Watson was holding a hand mirror in front of her, asking, "Is it to your liking, Miss Wendy?" This was a new game: Movie Star and her Entourage. No big mystery where they got that.

Mark stopped what he was doing to watch them, both of them sitting on a barstool to enjoy the show. A thought occurred to him at that very moment. "Where's Wilson?"

Bluebell looked around her, "I don't hear him."

"He's so quiet, he blends into the furniture. He could be anywhere." They both got up and crept around slowly, as if they were afraid he'd be spooked and run off into the woods. "He did wake up with the others, right? I'm not sure which kids I fed and which I didn't." The perils of having four identically sized children.

"He's up. I remember because he wanted to pick out his own shirt. It's red," no mystery where *he* got that, "so it shouldn't be too tough to spot. I'll take upstairs, you take down."

The pair split up in stealth mode, using army signals to indicate a game plan without disturbing the already occupied children. Bluebell crept upstairs and Mark tip-toed through the kitchen toward the family room. Just then he smelled it, the distinct odor of cigarette smoke, and his worst fear came to pass. A man, a cigarette smoking man, had snatched Wilson from his very own home, like in the movies, and all that remained was his rancid stench. "BLUEBELL! COME DOWN HERE!" he panicked.

Throwing open the back door to the yard Mark hollered his son's name at a volume he didn't previously know he was capable of, at an octave higher than he later cared to admit. Bluebell was only a few steps behind him, "You smell that?" Mark nodded. They followed the stink to a small corner near the water meter where they normally stored a cache of rakes this time of year. Right now though it was storing a small boy sitting nice and compact against the wall, who was presently trying frantically to stub out a cigarette against the siding.

"WILSON FRANCIS, WHAT DO YOU THINK YOU'RE DOING?" Bluebell was at the end of her rope, her voice less Mom and more lioness.

Mark bent down to grab the cigarette from Wilson's tiny fingers. His son's eyes shot open big and wide on full alert, realizing the gravity of being caught in one of his household's sworn mortal sins. No markers in the family room, take stairs one at a time, no touching the hot water knob on the bathroom faucet, matches stay in the kitchen junk drawer, and under no circumstances are they as a member of that family allowed to ingest anything inorganic. This meant that Aubergine's McDonalds wrappers didn't even make it into the house the night before. She ate in the car and tossed all evidence. Bluebell demanded it.

"Sorry, Daddy," his little voice trembled between the enraged noises coming from the mouths of his parents. Mark, usually the calmer of the two, felt a vein in his neck bulge and get hot and his attempt at words turned into an unintelligible series of grunts and puffs.

Bluebell grabbed Wilson by the shoulders. "Where did you get the cigarettes, Wilson? Who gave this to you?"

Wilson pled the fifth, stared at his feet.

"This isn't optional, Wilson. You answer me this instant. Who gave this to you?" Over her shoulder Mark held the butt in his hand like a baby bird, stretched away from his body, afraid of contaminating the evidence.

Wilson again refused and looked into her crazed face patiently. He'd learned by watching his siblings that if he just denied them the answer they were looking for, they'd give up asking eventually. Through their trial and error, Wilson got to be the envelope pusher with very little consequence besides the occasional time-out. Parenting books called it "testing his boundaries." Wilson called it "finding their weaknesses."

Bluebell stood and faced Mark. "Well, obviously it's Aubergine. I'll yell at her, you take Wilson upstairs."

Mark took his orders, "Upstairs, Mister. March." Little Wilson got on his feet and wiped his bottom. "NOW," Daddy barked. On the way inside Mark could be heard at his most level-headed as expected saying, "What do we say about our bodies, Wilson?"

Obediently Wilson answered, "That our bodies are temples where even God worships."

Bluebell took a second to contain herself, realizing if she walked in the house that moment that her kids would be witness to her frenzy. *Shove it out*, she decided, if even temporarily. A few deep breaths and after kicking a patio chair, hard, she attacked the stairs on the way up to the guest room.

"Unbelievable," Bluebell said aloud over her sleeping, buzz-saw sister. "Get. Up."

Aubergine snorted face down, waking a lot more abruptly than she would have preferred. For the third morning in a row she couldn't remember where she was upon opening her eyes. She rubbed her face and realized she'd gone to bed in her church/jail clothes, not even bothering to brush her teeth. She looked up and saw her sister standing, lips tight like a new catcher's mitt, arms crossed, a hip cocked to the side. "Morning?"

Bluebell's tone was deceptively placid, but inside her heart beat out of control. "I'm going to ask you this once."

Aubergine sat up to face her, one eye still closed. Her pants had ridden up in the middle of the night, creating a suffocating vacuum seal around her crotch region, ironic for her. She yanked them out of her butt and said, "Go for it."

"What in the Lord Jesus Christ's holy name would possess you to give a," yelling now, "FOUR YEAR OLD A CIGARETTE?" Her lips quivered and she felt an immediate shame for losing her cool.

Aubergine smiled. This was just perfect. "Bluebell, I don't smoke. I haven't had a cigarette since I spent those three months at that ashram. My body is clean," she swept her hand down her body as though suggesting purity flowed through her loins unhindered.

"You had four Old Fashioneds before one in the afternoon yesterday."

"It was a Sunday in Wisconsin, Bluebell. It's the law." Only half untrue.

"Is this a joke to you? My son was just sneaking a cigarette."

"Yes, this is actually hilarious to me. This is *priceless*. Because I didn't feed your goddamn son cigarettes, you lunatic." She grinned confidently. "I don't smoke, and therefore I don't have any to give to him. You're barking up the wrong tree, and you're so close to getting hit in the face. So, yes. It's hilarious to me."

"You know damn well I can kick your ass." Finally, remnants of her immaturity peeking through that contained exterior.

"I'd love to see you try, Suburbia," Auby mocked,

"Don't test me, Sissy."

"Excuse me, but there's a boy out there with an Apple logo imprinted into his forehead because of me. You really want to go?" Truth be told, Aubergine wasn't scared of much, but she was scared of her sister. She'd learned to bluff well over the years.

Luckily the feeling was mutual, and Bluebell left the room to find her real target.

"SLAM!" the door said, and the house shuddered at the thought of her unhinged.

The Rotation

It wasn't all misery. The plastics union secured
Frank quite the little retirement. Being a war veteran he got
the job with no hassle, and all the respect in the world from
his coworkers, without even having to complete his
application. It sat in his file without all the important
signatures for his entire tenure there. No one bothered to
make sure he'd checked the necessary boxes. They wanted
him, and that felt good. A lot of guys back from the war
weren't given the same red carpet.

After a couple of years there, upper management
noticed Frank never seemed to get tired, and despite being
paid by the hour and not piecework, was the highest
producing employee on the floor. In a sea of matching
coveralls and plastic caps, he was conspicuous, like one of
those old-timey movies that appeared sped up against the
real world pace around him. Luckily for Frank, this was the
sort of plant that rewarded hard work, not bled him of his
labor and let him die on the factory floor. He was promoted
to manager of something-or-other faster than anyone had,
all without a college education. The Marquette kids made
sure to remind him of that whenever they could, and vice
versa.

Frank was a competitive guy, so it was no wonder
that this kind of stand-out performance fed his masculinity.
The plant was great at making him feel like he was part of
something important, that there were hospitals that
depended on their output, even though he knew their

biggest profits came from disposable forks, knives, and spoons, and therefore their real contribution to the world was ensuring the feasibility of the backyard barbeque. Long live potato salad.

But he blocked that part out, for as long as he could. Walking in the door and seeing Lorraine at home with little Bluebell, who was less little every day, was victory enough for now. They'd just closed on their new house in a cozy little corner of the world, in the house they would have to die in in order to justify what he'd paid for it. It would serve as their hotel, their restaurant, their vacation getaway, and eventually their tomb if he was really going to get his money's worth.

None of that mattered on moving day, when Lorraine's take on things couldn't be any clearer. She seemed to be dancing through the rooms, Bluebell on her heels, a shuffle step every few beats, a butt wiggle at the discovery of her very own bedroom, a shimmy shimmy shimmy finding a laundry chute at the top of the stairs. "Just think of the stuff we can throw down there!" They spoke in songs for that entire day, and every day until the boxes were knocked down and used as sleds in their new backyard. Frank had given this family its dream come true, even if it was at the hands of his own.

Lorraine did what heavy lifting she could, but mostly just directed the boys where to put everything. Roscoe and Floyd, the brothers Frank never had, took the day to help out and did what they could to put his mind at ease that this was the right decision. "Take a look at this crown molding, Frank. What a beaut'!"

Frank hung onto them any way he could, they being his link to that artist world he missed. They were kind enough to straddle Frank and Lorraine's provincial living and the late-night rock and roll scene just to keep him alive, although even that was trailing off year after year, seeing them a little less every month, like an ellipses on his life…

Eventually they were settled in and the apartment was a shuttered memory Lorraine pretended never happened. She had something Frank didn't, which was the ability to live in her current state when she wanted to. She could turn it on and off like a light switch.

Frank's memories were like molten metal though, a fungible mass of events he couldn't separate from his today. When he thought wistfully about the Swingin' Door, he had to remind himself to think about his family's smiling faces, too. His joy cancelled out his pain, but then the reverse was true, too.

"Blue starts school soon," Lorraine mentioned over dinner one night. It was a fair trade. Frank gave up his soul's one true happiness, she made him dinner every night for the rest of his life.

"Yep, our girl's growing up."

Bluebell smiled at her peas. She could feel her parents stroking her cheek even when they weren't.

"She's special, Frank. She's going to be a queen."

"As long as this queen can read," he smirked at his daughter. "I really like this, Lorraine," pointing to his weird meat. "You should make this again."

"You got it. Consider it part of the rotation." Lorraine stopped eating, rested her chin in her palm. "What are you most excited for at school, Bluebell?"

She shrugged. How was she supposed to know? It's like being excited for life on Mars.

"I suppose you don't know what to expect. Well, I will tell you, your first day of school only happens once, so try and remember everything. *Everything*. And when you come home we can write a poem about it, so you can have that memory forever and ever." Bluebell loved when her mother talked like that. In her imagination behind her parents' shut bedroom door, her mother slept with a parakeet on her finger, squirrels snoozed at her feet, all on a bed made of rainbow colored music notes. Bluebell cherished her mother's unyielding whimsy.

Frank did, too, even if it was nuts.

"So what are you going to do to fill your time now?" Frank asked offhandedly.

She turned her attention to her husband. "Haven't decided yet."

Frank's pay had grown so substantially that she hadn't worked at the diner, or anywhere for that matter, in two years. Caring for Bluebell had been her full time job, doting her part time job, and Frank didn't doubt how time consuming that could be. He acknowledged what went on behind the scenes to make his life look effortless, and he was careful and appreciative of that. Other husbands he knew didn't have the benefit of Roscoe and Floyd and their forward thinking perspectives as influence on them.

Every stage had a crew to build it. Every character had a costume designer. His job was to play his part convincingly.

"It will be nice," Lorraine said, stretching out her arms and legs like a plank, "to get a nap in the middle of the day sometime." She smiled boastfully.

"Yes that will," Frank responded with an eyebrow.

"Have you ever thought about where you'd be right now if you never got injured? You could still be over there. You could be dead. You could be a brain injury in a hospital somewhere." Lorraine was full of subtle reminders.

"Sometimes I think I am," Frank stared into his plate. "Maybe this is all a figment. Maybe I had my brain rattled over there, and this is all happening in my head. And neither of you exist." An ominous film fell over his face. "Maybe I'm in a coma and you two are just neuron flashes." He looked at Bluebell, busily parting her vegetables into perfect grids, like an aerial view of bordering farms. "What do you think, Blue? Are you a neuron flash?"

"Sure, Daddy."

"Well, I have to say, if this is something your brain dreamed up, this says a lot about your subconscious," Lorraine said, a smile on her face, a darkness in her eyes. She could never hide that juxtaposition, no matter how good an actress she was. "People are all about their subtext, aren't they?"

Frank had to agree with her. This all could be one of two things. Either this was happening in his mind, and in his truest self he couldn't escape the human condition of never being satisfied, of taking a home in the suburbs and an opportunity for lifetime employment and only seeing it for the bottomless pit of subservience, loneliness, and feral sort of muscle-memory living it was.

Or else, if this wasn't some warped fantasy his subconscious conjured, this could only be his reality.

The room sighed.

Frank

The Astro Van screeched up to the Forty Winks
Inn in a way discouraged by GM. Bluebell took the turn so
hard and tight it looked like the van portion was going to
detach from the axle like a lid and go flying off into the
street. Wilson smacked his head on the window and
yawped, "Ouch, Mommy!"

"Sorry, baby, that's called centrifugal force." She
was poised as ever, on a mission. "We'll look it up in the
encyclopedia when we get home."

Wilson was scared, unused to seeing his mom with
road rage, or any rage. His world was pretty soft, pretty
much safe no matter what. Here was his mother though,
white knuckles and the music muted, hair in every direction
except where it usually went, with an eerie sense of calm
control.

When they parked Tim was already waiting in the
doorway, roused by the high-pitched squeal the van made
careening around the bend. Bluebell got out and charged up
to her brother without cutting the ignition or bothering to
even shut the door. He was terrified.

"Don't say a word, Timothy Gladney. I'm coming
here against all my better judgment as it is." Tim steadied
himself for her speech, waved at Wilson in the van,
puzzled. "My options were to bar you from having any
contact with my children whatsoever, or to denounce you to
them any time your name was brought up, or I could bring
Wilson here and have him correct your error so that he, and

possibly you, could actually learn something from all this. The last thing I need is my son associating your name with substance abuse." A vein in her neck was thick and taut under her skin.

"Substance abuse?!" Tim laughed. Bluebell was hilarious on every level to him, the same way homeless people who talked to themselves made him laugh.

She geared up for this one, her lips curling around the edges in a half human-half beast sort of snarl. "Cigarettes, Tim. Cigarettes!" He noticed how red she was all of a sudden. "He was smoking this morning. A cigarette you gave to him. *You.*"

"I didn't," *Shit*, he thought to himself, "I mean, I smoked near him, but I would never…" Tim felt awful. Even he knew four years old was too young to self medicate.

"Yeah, that's right. You ruined him. Do you know that since the second my beloved siblings made it across state lines, you've brought nothing but stress and torment to our lives? I told Mark how wonderful it would be," gesturing theatrically, a touch of her mother shining through, "to have you back here so we can grieve together. Instead all I've done is mother you two, and it has to stop." Nearing a full-scale implosion, "It has to stop, Tim. I can't," her face now in her hands, "I can't take this. Not now." She was exhausted.

He wasn't a robot. Seeing his sister in this state, and justifiably so, brought him to his knees every time. That's a fraction of the reason he left in the first place, albeit a very small fraction. Letting others down came easily to him, and this wasn't a family that pretended that was okay. "I'm sorry, Sissy," he pulled her to him. She clutched onto the maze of chains dangling off his pants and wept into his chest. "Leave him with me. I'll fix this." Bluebell looked him in the eye for any hint of bullshit. "I'm serious, I've got this. I want to make it right."

In a few minutes Tim and Wilson were sitting together on his double bed in the Forty Winks Inn, not completely understanding what either of them was supposed to say, or why Bluebell had trusted him to articulate some sort of moral of the story.

"You have your own TV?" Wilson asked, his attempt at breaking the ice.

"Don't change the subject, buddy."

Wilson looked down at his hands and waited for the right words to come. Nothing did. Best to sit and take it.

"Kid, do you know why your mom dropped you off here?"

He shrugged. "To punish me?"

"Not exactly. She's pissed off that you smoked this morning. It scared her. And yeah, she's angry." Wilson nodded, looked at him with those giant, innocent eyes. "Do you know why she's so angry?" Again, he nodded. "Because smoking is bad for you. It's so bad for you, Wilson. I don't know how to make you understand that, because you're just a little kid and you have no perspective." Tim tried to find something Wilson could relate to. "You ever had a pet?" Wilson shook his head. "A rat? Nothing?" Nope. "No pets ever?"

"Mommy says I have to wait till I'm mur-ture enough."

"Well, this is going to set you back a couple of years, just so you know." Tim stood up and paced, realizing at that moment how hard it is to get a point across to a baby child with baby child thought processes. "Okay, you love your sister, right?" Wilson thought about it. "You're right. Forget that. Think of someone you love more than anything. Maybe that's your dad, maybe it's one-eared Raymond. I don't give a shit."

"Language."

Tim ignored him. "Take that person you love and imagine them being gone forever because of some stupid stuff they did to their body. You'd never see them again, because they decided they wanted to smoke cigarettes. That's awful, right? That a person would choose cigarettes over their best friend in the whole world? That's all your mom is getting crazy about. I mean, wouldn't you want her to take care of herself so that's she's always around?"

"So, why do you smoke, Uncle Tim?" Valid question.

"Because I'm an idiot, that's why." Wilson giggled. Tim was caught off guard by that. "Are you laughing? I don't think I've ever seen you laugh before. Kid your size should laugh a lot more than you do." He sat down next to Wilson and looked at their reflection in the television. "You've got a lot of people around you that love you very much, more than most people. You've got the best fuckin' family, like you won some kind of lottery. And if anything happened to you, it would hurt a lot people. You have to know that, okay? You have to be really aware of all the people you're hurting when you hurt yourself."

Tim had no idea if the kid really understood the concept, but it mattered to him that he got the words out.

It's a speech he'd repeated subconsciously all his life, just to keep himself from running off the rails.

Wilson put his little hand on Tim's and said softly, "Uncle Tim, there are people who love you, too."

Tim dissolved right into himself and fizzled like an Alka Seltzer tablet. "I appreciate that."

"I'm hungry."

"I could go for some pancakes. Some international ones. You want to walk down with me and get some mid-day breakfast?"

"Yes, please."

IHOP took good care of them that morning. Tim ordered the Smokehouse Combo, and when the waitress asked Wilson for his order, he answered, "That sounds nice. I'll have what he's having," even though he hadn't a clue what a Smokehouse Combo was a combo of. When their orders came, of the two pancakes, two sausage links, two eggs, and hash browns, Wilson was able to finish half a cake and one link.

"Think you got in over your head there?"

"Maybe," Wilson answered and burped down into his sweater. Might have also been a lot easier to eat had he removed his big puffy mittens before trying to grasp a fork with them. Tim thought Blue would have never allowed it, so he let the kid have one goofy meal in his life. When the waitress remarked on it, Tim cast her a grave glare and said, "His hands were burned in a house fire."

Without missing a beat, Wilson contributed, "I saved the cat." When she walked away in shock, Tim winked at the boy, a proud moment for them.

The meal seemed to be just what both of them needed. Wilson had been craving someone who would talk to him without it being a life lesson or an opportunity to lecture. Tim needed someone who knew nothing about his life up to this point and held no prejudices and made no assumptions. Who better than a four year old? In fact the only mention of Tim's unusual attire was Wilson complimenting him on his make-up. "You look like a wrestler."

Throughout their lunch conversation swayed from intense and reflective:

> "If you could change back and forth from an animal to a human any time you wanted, what would you be?" (Wilson: Saber Tooth Tiger, Tim: Hawk)

To light and breezy:

> "Once my mom was on the toilet and I heard her poop." (Tim's response, "Your mother is disgusting.")

To truly contemplative:

> "How come European musicians always sound American when they're singing? (Wilson's answer, "What's a yurpeen?")

Tim was delighted to hear Wilson was considering being a drummer when he grew up, or a CIA agent. "Both of those are fine career choices. Maybe you could do both."

"Be realith-tic, Uncle Tim."

In the end Tim polished off Wilson's plate for him, making monster slobbers, gobbles, and roars as he chugged the food back like a T-Rex. Wilson thought it might have been the funniest moment of his entire life.

"Let's get you back to your mother before she has a fucking conniption."

"Okay."

Afterward the boys loaded up in the Festiva. Tim had no idea Wilson was too small for the front seat, and so the little one got quite the treat that day, cruising the streets of Elm Grove like a big boy, despite not being able to see over the dashboard. It was chilly, but the sun heated his face through the windows, and his heart was warm. He couldn't think of a more fun day he'd ever had.

Pulling up to the house, Tim got out of the car to help unbuckle his nephew. He squatted on the passenger side and took advantage of this last moment of privacy with the kid. "You remember what I told you, Wilson. You've got some pretty good parents. Not a lot of kids do. Most parents suck. My parents sucked. But if you had to go shopping for parents, yours are the ones you'd want to pick. So go easy on them, okay? Do what they say. They're really smart."

Wilson put a hand on Tim's shoulder and leaned in close, sympathizing. "Your parents sucked?"

"Yeah. Grandma and Grandpa weren't exactly naturals."

"Gramma and Grampa? Gramma Lorraine?" Wilson appeared to be horrified by this accusation.

"Yep, and Grandpa Frank."

Wilson couldn't believe his ears. Grandma and Grandpa were his next best outlet other than his new friend Uncle Tim, and with Frank passing away only a few days prior, Tim's unkind words weren't sitting well with him. "Grampa Frank taught me how to box."

"Really? Because he taught me how to gamble the mortgage money."

"Grampa was a hero in 'Nam."

"I highly doubt that."

"Grampa took me to a Packer game."

"Grandpa burned my Packer tickets when he was drunk."

"Grampa can speak German."

"He was faking it."

"Grampa almost saved Kennedy's life at his athathinathon, but the CIA wouldn't let him."

"Grandpa lied to you. He was just a kid in the sixties."

"Grampa named his parrot after me."

"Well, I hate to tell you this, kid, but I was just at Grandpa's house, and there was no parrot there. So he probably ate it."

Wilson felt what it really meant to be angry. Tears shot down his face, his lower lip blubbered, but he didn't feel any of it. "You don't talk about my Grampa like that. He's a good Grampa."

"Maybe, Wilson. But he was a shitty dad." It was at that moment Tim realized that back in the motel, when he asked Wilson to imagine someone he really loved, he was imagining Grampa Frank.

Wilson couldn't take this blasphemy and bum rushed his uncle, not to harm him, but to get away as quickly as possible. Tim fell back from his squat into the gravel as the kid flew past him to the front door. Bluebell just happened to be coming outside to greet them, but Wilson buzzed by her in a gust of wind, tears frozen to both cheeks.

Tim finally found his feet to see his sister with her hands outstretched. "You gotta be kidding me."

Tim didn't know where to begin. "I think that one's broken," he called back to her.

Revelations

"**Well**, speak of the devil. Satan herself," Tim announced from the sofa. Just as Bluebell was completing scolding him, he could see out the bay window that Mother was pulling up to the house in her 1978 yellow Mercedes Benz convertible, the top down, in November. Blue stood in an archway with her hands on her hips, bushed. It had indeed been a trying week for her. She was suddenly parent to two grown adults. Wilson, the triplets, and now twins.

"Mother's here?"

"GRAMMA!" all four children rang out in unison, their feet tick-tacking along the hard woods like puppies trying to maneuver a sharp corner.

"She has the timing of a cold sore," Tim said jovially.

The door thrust open with a force unconcerned with the small children that might be barreling toward it. "My lovelies!" she entered, and smothered each and every child like a circus bear who didn't know her strength. She was all paws and kisses, more affection than Tim had seen in his lifetime.

"Gramma, we missed you!"

"Gramma, I made a birthday card for myself!"

"Gramma, my toe hurts!"

"Gramma, did you bring food for the squirrels?"

"Gramma, is your car a space ship?"

"Gramma, I ate asparagus last night!"

"Gramma, is Jesus a cat?"

"Gramma, my daddy said a curse word!"

"Gramma, I can't read yet!"

All overlapping, like a really loud quilt.

"Oh, really? Did you write 'To Wendy, Love Wendy?'...Yes, Wilson, there are breadcrumbs and rum candies in my purse...Asparagus? Gross!...You know, I'm not sure. Maybe he's a cat, maybe he's a professional basketball player. Nobody really knows...". Tim marveled at how she handled them. He was overwhelmed just observing this pint-sized attack. But Mother was magnanimous. She ate it up. "Now, what did I say about your suffocating me when I first arrive?"

All together in sing-song intonation, "Three inches of space, pleeeaase."

"That's right, children, just until I am settled in," she responded, loosening her scarf, like a haughty queen.

Mark entered the room, the loyal subject. "Mother is the name for God in the lips and hearts of little children."

"Hello, there, Wordsmith. Come here and give Lorraine a big kiss on the mouth," which he dutifully planted on her. She gave his backside a good swat like a football coach.

Mark appeared to enjoy her company, confusing the hell out of Tim. He remembered a Japanese horror film where a child was seduced into kissing a bunny rabbit, but when she opened her eyes the bunny had morphed into a dragon, and the child's hair and eyebrows were singed off by the dragon's fiery breath. Before the child could react she was eaten whole. *Run, Mark. Run*, Tim begged from the inside.

"Where do you come up with these magnificent greetings?" Mother asked, a postcard of a woman.

"I've got a million of 'em," Mark answered, tapping his temple. Tim felt his pancakes inching up the back of his throat, a mix of gut and maple syrup.

Bluebell cast a glance Tim's way, as if to say, *See?*

"I think I read this in Revelations," Tim said to no one in particular.

"Oh, Timothy, I didn't see you there. I thought you were a shadow."

"No. I exist."

Saved by the bell, Tim heard the welcome ring of Aubergine's Blackberry as she thumped down the stairs. Reaching the bottom, she froze at the sight of Mother's paisley caftan, fluttering in the breeze she created just by talking with her hands. It felt like an ambush. This reminded her of the time she awoke in an Oxnard hotel room to find her agent, manager, and producer at the foot of the bed, pitching rehab to her. It was an intervention designed to revive her career, but she resented it as much as an intervention designed to save her life.

"Oh. You're all here," Mother said to Bluebell coldly, acknowledging her middle child with a flash of eye contact that burned right through them both.

Aubergine wouldn't dignify the dig, decided she'd had bad enough a 24-hours to give Mother any of the remaining energy she had left. "Tim, that was Gerard on the phone. Want to go get drunk?"

"Bluebell, darling, did you hear that? Your sister has been in town for two days and already has a date with what sounds like a responsible young man. And nine of those hours were spent in the big house. Impressive!" By now Mother was making her way into the kitchen to adore her grandchildren, leaving her insults behind her like the stench of death.

"You told her? Jesus, Bluebell, what good could that have served?"

"I didn't know who else to call. I was worried."

"You suck."

Mother hollered from the other room, "Aubergine, are you going to run a comb through your hair? Or is this a desperate cry for help?" The kids giggled off in the distance. Tim could see from his vantage point them perched at her feet, like she was breeding a litter of sycophants.

Bluebell begged with her eyes, but Aubergine wasn't interested in that game. "Tim, coming?" He rose without saying a word, Auby grabbed her great big purse, and the two jingled out the front door. "You're welcome," she said once the door shut behind them.

Tim tapped his cigarette box into his palm like a pardoned inmate. "Who the fuck's Gerard?"

The Boat

Inevitably, Frank's mind went back to Vietnam. In the stillness of Lorraine's dead-log sleeping, he sometimes worried she wasn't breathing, and his mind went to other places.

At this point in America's nasty break-up with Vietnam, the people who knew about his history there lauded his safe return as the best thing that could have happened to him, one way or another. Some people said it with their eyes, other people came right out and told him, as though they understood. He liked to laugh at those people, because they were so worldly, so road weary in what they thought were their big lives.

Frank couldn't hate them. They didn't know. They pitied what he'd seen with his eyes and done with his hands as though it damaged his little warrior psyche. To him though, the height of living is almost dying. To be able to reach out and touch that tenuous filament between safety and catastrophe is to truly respect it. But these kids who worked under him, some above him, their deaths were so far off from the plastics plant, it was an abstruse possibility, not a fact. To those kids it was like understanding the reaches of the universe. No point in wondering what's out there if they'll never see it themselves.

What a comfortable existence, but what's the point in that? A few horrors came to mind from time to time, usually popping in as reminders on the evening news, once looking too deep into a pan of Lorraine's meatloaf, and he would shudder a little, thinking about his guys. But mostly he felt a longing for it. He asked himself if he would go back if given the chance, a hypothetical conversation with his psyche. Always the answer was no. It didn't take a minute to come to that conclusion. But he missed the fear.

At night he often sat up and peered around their bedroom, with that sort of night vision you only get in the depths of the sleeping hours, where you could practically read a book using just the light coming in from streetlamps. It was like he took stock. Family: *check*. Home: *check*. General security: *check*. It was all there. A seven year old who still asked him to teach her things, a semi-annual vacation up to Door County, a paunchy neighbor who he could talk football scores with, even though they owned no TV and hadn't seen a game since he was 20. He faked it. But it was all there. Everything that was supposed to satisfy him.

Looking at Lorraine, flat like a pancake, out like a light, he wondered if this was what she envisioned all those years before. Did she fall into it, too? Or did she engineer this on purpose? If not, if it was all an accident that they'd abandoned their bohemian existence and all the unpredictability of it, was that why she was pulling away from him? He couldn't blame her if so. He was sleepwalking through most of the day anyway. Sometimes he was hit with the bolt of reality that it wasn't all her doing, and he'd look down at his feet and realize she was at the dock, and it was *his* little boat built for one slowly drifting out to the middle of Lake Michigan, where no one could touch him.

Despite Lorraine being the only person he could wake at that hour and talk about his slightly unhealthy affection for the fear of death, the only person who would sit and listen and understand what his life was lacking, that he missed music, that he missed the rush of the stage, that he missed any rush whatsoever, he still let that boat drift. Perhaps it was because she understood already, and yet still this was their life, that he wanted to get away from her without leaving a ripple in the water.

In this low-lit room, Frank watched the clock. *Tick...tick...tick.* He couldn't hear it, but he felt it beat in time with his fading heart.

Womb Bats

"**A** silver Festiva, Tim?" Gerard joked dryly.

"It's gray, actually."

Night time came sometime after four this time of
year, a period before Thanksgiving when a breed of
Milwaukeean was reborn, or died, depending on how you
thought of it. In the summer the typical Wisconsinite can be
seen grilling, mowing, frisbeeing, swimming, playing any
number of sports in the city streets, anything that can
possibly be done outdoors, and from the crack of dawn past
nine at night. Neighbors compete for best lawn patterns,
debate the virtue of using cherry wood versus composite to
build their decks, and the line at the boat launch is an hour
and a half long on a Tuesday afternoon. Grateful for the
warmth and the long days, the state of Wisconsin uses their
homes for cooking and sleeping only. For a few insatiable
months they are sun kissed and righteous.

But then the first chill comes toward the end of
September, the first cold day in October, and the first
consistent streak of ass-clenching freeze in November.
December is worse, January unbearable, February cruel and
unusual, March one more gray day away from a nervous
breakdown. Knowing what's coming, November is the
realization that all is lost. Life has to begin again indoors.
No more gardens. No more halter tops. Sunglasses find
their way underneath the driver's seat to be forgotten about
for all eternity. Merriment sits in a waiting line behind
yawns and sighs. Skin slowly loses its lizardy armor and

mutes into a translucent, itchy sort of wonton wrapper. Cheeks lose their glow. Optimism is flimsy, hope a soggy square of toilet paper.

Not much to do other than drink. The excuse is that it is protection from the cold, but the optimal word should be distraction. Wisconsin is the only state in the union that still allows children to legally drink alcohol in the company of their parents, and it isn't unusual to find entire families in bars, baby carrier perched next to their pitchers of MGD. The alcohol tolerance of these people is mythical, their fortitude, in what Southern states would consider inhospitable conditions, is that of legend. Something about the dearth of sun, the excess of beer, the dry, calloused handshakes, it all makes for a highly contemplative, sentimental people. Grown men sit in ice fishing shacks and talk about their high school football glory in one frosty breath, their long lost loves in another, all before killing and eating a nine-point buck with only their bare hands. It ain't for the faint of heart.

This particular day the men and their mother issues lined the bar at Ryan's Public House, a bar Aubergine remembered from her childhood. Tim was smaller back then, but he was there in her memory, too. When Bluebell went off to college there was no one around to watch them anymore, so the jukebox and spare darts laying around the bar entertained them enough to let Frank and Lorraine fight in public, as opposed to home.

"This is why I got out, Gerard. Because one of these guys could have been someone I was sleeping with. Regularly." She took a sip of her drink. "Okay, it's one of the reasons." Aubergine used the words "why I got out" about every hour on the hour since stepping foot in Wisconsin. She couldn't find a kind word to say about the place.

Gerard signaled the young goateed man serving them. "Barkeep, can we get some shots here?"

Tim and Aubergine spewed the obligatory "I really shouldn't/No way, man/Too rich for my blood" sort of protests. But Gerard knew this was as cultural a nuance as belching after an Indian meal, and took their refusals as hearty appreciation.

"My treat, so my pick. Let's do three shots of Jägermeister, please."

Aubergine pulled her baseball cap low. She was three drinks in and already a touch paranoid. Adding Jäger to this class act might attract some unwanted attention. "Gerard, I'm, like, twenty minutes out of jail. Isn't Jäger an opiate?"

Goatee pulled the licorice liqueur out of the mini-fridge and poured three tall shots.

"Can I get a straw?" Tim joked. "This might kill me."

"Come on, you pussies. You've been gone too long. Raise 'em up," Gerard demanded, ever the shaper of young alcoholics, "Here's to…anyone?"

Tim cleared his throat, "Here's to coming home. Because it's important to be reminded why you shouldn't." CLINK! And down the gullet it went.

"One more of these and I'm pantless," Auby declared. Her Milwaukee was starting to show, like the hint of a slip under her skirt.

Gerard hiccupped, blew out a burp. Aubergine laughed, noticed his humanity for the first time in her life.

It took her until that moment to feel like she was sitting next to anyone besides her high school music teacher. "You're a *real person*, Mr. Leeney. You know? It's weird." Aubergine's awareness for her drunkenness always grew at the same rate her vocabulary declined.

"Right. I know. Like when you first realize your parents once had sex. I know. I get it all the time. I'm sure this is how your fans feel when they see you shopping at Target. It's like, oh, yeah, she needs deodorant and toilet paper sometimes, too."

Tim added, "When your neighbors catch you without your make-up."

"Yeah, what's that about?" Gerard asked. "What's the strategy behind this image of yours?"

"Let's see. If I'm sober, I say something along the lines of 'It's my job as a renegade to test what people will stomach.'" Tim and alcohol had exactly the opposite marriage Aubergine had with it. His eloquence grew by the pint glass. "But when I've had a few, my reasoning is that it's an effort to get my mother's attention. I provoke her. It's Oedipal. I'm perfectly aware of it."

Gerard was impressed. "All the way from Portland you provoke her?"

"Childhood demons are bigger than state borders, man." He signaled the bartender for three more. "I'm working on it."

Aubergine slobbered, "Yeaaaah, right. How are you working on it?"

"Same as you, Auby. Through my music."

"You moron, my music is not my..."

Gerard helped her out, "Your therapy."

"Right. My music is my escape," she said, waving her hands through an imaginary world in the atmosphere above her eye line.

Tim refused to capitulate, "I'm not going to give you this one. Your music is an effort to gain our parents' approval. Mine is an effort to stoke the fire, express my inner shit. Get it out of me so it can't damage me anymore."

Aubergine tried to get her head to process that. "That might be the smartest I've ever heard you talk."

"What's your band called?" Gerard inquired.

"The Womb Bats."

Gerard laughed, slapped a hand on the bar top, then realized he was the only one amused. "You were serious, my apologies. Well, that name is compelling. Would you say you are a bat from your mother's womb? Or do the bats represent your mother's inability to be maternal? What's the symbolism there?"

"I just thought it was a funny way to pronounce 'wombats.' And it looks kind of hardcore with our logo." Tim drew a pentagram with bat wings on a cocktail napkin. Gerard admired it. "You like death metal, Gerard?"

"I'm more of a classic rock kind of guy."

"That's too bad. In our encore we all cut into our skin and bleed onto the stage. Our fans go apeshit over it."

"Batshit," Gerard corrected.

"Right."

"Wow," Gerard didn't know what to say. Certainly nothing encouraging.

"We always end with 'Alive Enough to Die.' It's fucking beautiful. Girls cry. It's Shakespearean."

"Sounds like a fun romp," Gerard remarked.

"I was on Oprah once, you know," Aubergine butted in. The three shots arrived finally, and this time she didn't wait for any formal toast. "I had it all." *Slurp*, the shot the warm hug she needed at that point. "Eminem drunk dialed me. Twice." Wiping the shot off the corners of her mouth, "My abs were featured in a segment on Entertainment Tonight. They put my photo next to Mount Rushmore and said we were separated at birth." She sensed Tim and Gerard working too hard to make the connection. "Because I'm rock hard, you see. Or I was when it aired." She signaled the bartender for three more shots. "I got a standing 'O' at the MTV Video Music Awards. Paris Hilton poured a drink on me. I was IT. But where'd all that go?" She spit a little of her nausea into a nearby ashtray. "See how they fucked us, Tim? Because of Mother and Father, you haven't washed your hair in months."

Gerard tried to inconspicuously sneak a look at the grease in Tim's hair. It had a dull sheen to it.

"I sabotaged my own career," she continued. The next three shots arrived, the bartender having no qualms about over-serving. Christmas was coming after all, and drunk people tended to tip more. She blathered something incomprehensible, "Music…front row at Michael Kors…rosary beads…FUCKING AGENTS!...suck ass Mother…" and then appeared to have an idea. "Let's call her."

"I don't think that's a good idea," Gerard tried to calm her, albeit with terrified eyes.

"Let's do it," Tim confirmed.

"Never, ever call someone in this state. You know this won't turn out well."

"Gerard, our mother already wrote us off. How much worse could she think of us? Come on, we can call your ex-wife next. Fuck her!" Adrenaline shot through her like the first time she met and subsequently made out with the Asian guy she thought might have been Jet Li.

"That won't be necessary," writing an imaginary signature in the air, hoping the bartender saw him.

Aubergine's Blackberry seemed to pop up out of nowhere, always at the ready, like a gunslinger and his .44, and Tim hopped off his barstool. "Do you have her number?"

Auby scrolled through her contacts to the name, "Lorraine." So many years she'd contemplated deleting the number all together, but the pull stopped her every time, that pull to one day be able to call Mother and hear love on the other end. In a more sober state, better judgment convinced her that would never be. Her heart beat violently. "What should we say?"

"Guys, there's a reason why they make those keys so small. To make it as hard as possible to do what you're about to do."

"I'll take that as a challenge," Aubergine dared. She was salivating. She hit the "send" button without another thought, and on the other end the phone rang and rang, a good thirty seconds or so. She grew impatient, felt her nerve slipping.

"She's obviously not there. Just hang up," Gerard prayed for a malfunctioning answering machine.

But Tim egged her on, "She doesn't have a machine. She's there. The first ring or two she spent cursing. And the next couple squeezing out her ass out of her chair. And the next couple waddling over to the phone. She's there."

"Hallo," Lorraine answered on the other end. Hollow. Kurt. Morose.

Aubergine froze.

"Hallo?"

Auby shook her head, panicked, held the handset out for Tim to say anything. Gerard heaved relief and his shoulders collapsed.

"HALLO? Anybody there?"

Tim whispered, "What the fuck, Sissy. Handle this."

But Aubergine wimped out. She set the phone on the bar top and stepped away trying not to disturb it. Gerard grabbed it, attempted to end the call but failed to find the button, those goddamn small keys. Eventually he ripped off the back plate and tore out the battery.

"You pussy," Tim scolded, in exactly the tone their mother used too many times with her.

Gerard slid the dismembered phone her way and tried to find any words to say. Tim slumped back onto his bar stool, finding only enough room in himself to be disappointed in his sister, and none enough to remember a second earlier he couldn't speak above ten decibels with the thought of his mother on the other line. Aubergine's brain emptied and she sat staring ahead like the sad, sallow creature she was.

The bartender, having overheard the scenario, slid the chit Gerard's way in a black leather book. "No rush, guys," staring Aubergine down a little closer. The burn of his inspection was too familiar. She yanked her hat off, shook out her hair and sat up a little straighter. *Fuck it*, she reasoned.

Gerard pulled out his wallet and found a card he knew would go through. "Listen, guys, I think you need to get to the point in your lives where you make the realization."

His audience turned to him, eager for wisdom, eager to be saved.

"You need to understand this sooner than later. You ready?" The Gladneys stared up at him eagerly. "There is no resolution. This is what we like to call 'adulthood.'" He used air quotes and maximum condescension. "Life is a series of unfinished business, and very, very little of it will ever be just. You think you're going to wake up and something is going to happen that will enlighten you, some discovery in the middle of the night, and you will be forever healed and changed, and birds will sing. I'm telling you, that does not happen. It just does not. Your life is not a movie, it is an abstract poem that doesn't rhyme. There's no plot, no hero, no arc. It is unpredictable and sucks most of the time. But this is it, my friends. Most poetry does suck. This is all you need to know."

He stepped away from the bar and continued. "You want resolution? Here's your resolution." He opened the little book and read the check, not missing a beat. "Do your life better than you're doing it now. That's it. Anything less than that is exhausting for the rest of us to watch."

The bartender ran Gerard's card while Tim and Aubergine soaked it all in quietly. The Jägermeister and the truth, one the underpinning for the other.

Two Bucks

"**Funeral** morn'," Tim said to himself, alone in his hotel room. He scratched his dirty hair and stood in his underwear, staring out the window. No view, just traffic moving at a disinterested pace. It was early, a hint of daytime, pre-rush hour. He had the window cracked so he could smoke a cigarette, and didn't much care who saw him there half naked.

What a perfect day to bury a body. The Festiva was covered in frost, and it being a West coaster, would take about a year to warm up and get him where he needed to go today. The streets had a slick gleam to them, and the sun was somewhere back there behind those heavy clouds. Everyone was anonymous in this weather. Anybody walking the streets was shrouded in a heavy parka or umbrella, everyone's head down. It was like looking at an impressionistic painting of his own subconscious.

Strangely these sorts of days comforted him. There was a certain freedom in being invisible. On the rare sunny day in Portland, Tim wore sunglasses everywhere, his last possible barrier between him and a normal relationship with anyone else in the world. He walked around in his life protected by his little disguise, listening to the beat of his breath and footsteps. He always felt he was less looking through his own eyes and more so through the lens of a camera. Everyone was on the other side of the view finder, and he liked it that way.

Tim's mind hadn't bothered yet getting anywhere passed this moment. It was apparent he would have to say something, anything, in front of a lot of people. Father's spectrum of friends could be better classified as protégés, service workers, masochists, lovers perhaps? Not a single one, besides Mother, would be his soul's true connection to the world. In actuality, the people in that church would be saying goodbye to a stranger. Frank was his son's father after all. So what do you say about a stranger? What could he come up with that was both redeemable and not a total fabrication?

And the underlying question of course was whether or not he even owed it to his father to create the fable. All he could thank Frank for was the fact that he had sex with Lorraine one last time before checking out completely, and there were certainly plenty of days Tim doubted this was in fact a blessing and not a lifetime of discontent passed down, just for fun. Because that one night Frank was drunk and horny and Lorraine was willing. No magic. No fated meeting of egg and sperm. Just a basic primal urge, a chemical craving, a sweaty one at that. This was his genesis.

A half hour later his sabbatical at the Forty Winks Inn was over and Tim was zipping up his duffel bag. He put a gray wool tie in his pocket and decided he'd wait until arriving at the church to determine whether it was necessary to complete the look. He hated ties, all men hate ties, but he hated his sister's wrath more.

"Checking out," Tim slapped the key card down onto the reception desk. Percy, slovenly as ever, was halfway through a Big Gulp. Tim extended his hand in thanks.

"Leaving so soon? What the fuck, dude? We didn't even get to chill."

"Real life, man. Got to get back to real life."

"I thought you weren't leaving until after your dad's funeral."

"Yeah, that's," checking his watch, "in about an hour."

"No shit? Well you look real nice. You're going to knock 'em dead." Percy could be classified as Mark's polar opposite, horrible with words.

"Thanks, man. I'm supposed to stand up and say something. Figured I should probably not look like a total asshole."

"Wow. What are you going to say? That's a lot of pressure." Tim shook his head. "Can I tell you my favorite memory of your dad? You can use it in your story up there, if you want." Thank God. "I was at 711, and he was there, too. It was late and I had a craving for some Rice-a-Roni. I can't explain why, it was just a weird late night *desire* for some Rice-a-Roni."

"You were stoned?"

"Yeah, man. Anyway," talking with his hands, using the Big Gulp like a prosthetic limb, "he was there getting batteries or something. Maybe some beer or something. No, it was batteries, I remember. C Batteries. I was like, 'Mr. Gladney, what, are you juicing up your boom box and shit?' You know, fuckin' with him." Tim sighed, realizing this wasn't the story he was looking for. "So we're talking, you know, shooting the shit. Packers, whatever. So I bid my adieu and realize I don't have enough money. I was short by, like, two bucks. 711 charges an arm and a leg for some rice, let me tell you. So I'm at the counter pissed off at myself, because I'm realizing at this point that if I wasn't so damn high, I'd probably have remembered to bring at least fifty percent more money than I would normally, not to mention I'd probably be in bed or something and not up in the middle of the night with an uncontrollable compulsion for Rice-a-Roni."

"Right." Tim was trying to look intrigued.

"So I'm having this rice crisis, a rice-is," Percy smiled, pleased with himself, "when your dad cruises up to the counter like a bad ass. He's got his wallet out already, I don't even have to ask. Before I know it, he's got two bucks on the counter like it ain't no thing."

Tim paused, waiting for the climax to this historic event. "Then what?"

"I thanked him, he called me a faggot, and I left."

This was it? Percy's fondest memory of Frank Gladney was two bucks and gay slurs? This funeral was going to be harder than he'd expected, and for all the wrong reasons. He was going to have to delicately straddle the line between not caring nearly enough to emote in any way, but caring enough not to offend his sister, or any other fool who might be grieving. It would be perilous territory purposely offending Mother while protecting Bluebell and the Ws.

"Hey, dude, you want me to go with you? A little moral support?" Percy was wearing a heathered gray zip-up hoodie that was just opened enough to reveal a t-shirt that Tim could see read "I eat more pussy than Alf."

"No. But thank you. You take care, Percy." One more handshake and he was out the door.

"Flap those wings, Glad-Bag!" Percy saluted with the wrong hand, but with all the affection in the world.

Posture

A few blocks away Bluebell was stirring. More specifically she was stirring a giant glob of mayonnaise into a macaroni salad, a steady stream of snot hindering her from getting anything done. Mark designated the basement as the holding pen for the kids. "Mommy needs to be alone this morning," he told them, and judging by the look on his face, it wasn't worth it to challenge him.

"I just can't stop crying," she complained, refusing to look up from her duties. After the funeral there would be a house full of people, hungry people, and not a single person had called to ask what they could bring. "There's only so much I can cook with all these boogers on my sleeve."

Mark took the spatula from her and shooed her away. It was his job after all, not the aching daughter. She found a dining chair near the window and took comfort in the mist blanketing her yard. It was soothing enough for her to sit and just stare into it. Sometimes the fog rolled along the grass like a slow moving train, but this early morning it lay there thick and stubborn, like a force field protecting her from the heaviness of the day.

Her hair, *This goddamned hair*, she thought to herself, something she wouldn't dare say aloud and felt guilty enough even thinking. She got up before dawn to set it. It was hurricane proof, a shellacked sort of exoskeleton. For some reason she thought the day called for approximately 40% more hairspray than usual. Given the moisture in the air, it wasn't the worst idea, but her motivation was really just to provide a perfect day for her father. Perfect service, perfect food, perfect goddamned hair. Her lower lip sputtered like an old lawnmower, a build-up of tears giving way.

Bluebell took a deep breath, very deep, all the way down to her tailbone, and felt the stillness of being all filled up with air. The room was silent like death except for the sound of various utensils clinking and scraping a few feet away. Her cheeks puffed up and her face went red until she let it all out in an audible flatus. Her husband, the perfect husband, looked up with only his eyes and smiled at her, then went back to work. He would be doing no policing of her emotions on this day. The sky was the limit for her neurosis.

Upstairs her navy blue boat-neck dress, so smart looking and perfectly pressed, was laid out flat on her bed. At the bottom was a small ruffle. Father always preferred her to be girly. He said, "Girls are girls, and boys are boys, and the world will end when we finally can't tell the difference." Of course Mother always said, "Men are expendable, and it's important to remind them." It's a wonder Bluebell figured out how at all to behave. A little bit of Frank, a little bit of Lorraine, and out came a housewife with a consistent 115lb. frame, a Madison education, and the ability to change her own tire. She knew a little bit about everything, but not too much about any one thing. Expertise in any field but mothering was a masculine trait.

She put her head down on the dining room table and felt the cold against her cheek, shutting her eyes. There was something numbing about it. She could breathe a little shallower, relax her pout. Snot ran out of her nose faster than she could catch it, so she just let it go, dripping onto the table under her. Everything slowed, even the sounds around her. She could hear the distant cheers and growls of her children through the table like waves in a conch shell, but lower pitched than usual, like a cassette tape on its last leg. In a second she was asleep without any dreams, just a blank brain letting go. The only peace she'd known in years.

Then, as quickly as she fell asleep, her eyes snapped open in a panic. "Posture," she said out loud, and sprang up to a perfect ninety degree angle. Mother would never have approved.

Buffer

Upstairs Aubergine hid in the guest room. What a goddamn pain in the ass this day was going to be. Sometimes, all the time, it was just as well to operate on a completely unconscious level and let her childhood baggage lead the way. In her everyday life she only had to be so mature or diplomatic or considerate. On this particular morning though, once she left her room she would have to put on her "well adjusted" mask. She would have to be patient with her sister, tender with her, and completely block out the presence and commentary of her mother. Aubergine prayed masked men would rush in and hold up the church at gunpoint, just to put some perspective on things. *So what if Father's dead- I was just mugged!*

She had been dressed for a half hour, but still sat in the window seat upstairs, turning her lipstick over and over in her hand like a soldier would a bullet, a poker champ would a chip. She saw the mist from up high and prayed for other reprieves. Something torrential to blow in and suck the roof off the church. A stampede of bison maybe. This was impossible, of course. Bluebell wouldn't cancel if the church blew up. Aubergine accepted her fate, but for now would skip breakfast and wait for the "all aboard" before she surfaced.

She held up her compact and stared into her face for a second. She'd lost a bit of her tan in the few days she'd been gone from sunny California. It had only taken this small amount of time to deplete her of any life force left.

Her cheeks were pallid and gaunt, her eyes heavy with bags filled to the zipper with anxiety, her hair frizzy as shit. There was something about California weather that smoothed her long locks so that even when she didn't brush it, every curl looked intentional. Out here the moisture and the stress created a disheveled sort of haystack style. No amount of product could save this catastrophe of a head.

When Aubergine was in California her life was certainly uncertain. Or uncertainly certain. Sure, at the height of her fame things were all very chaotic. She couldn't so much as use a public restroom without a website reporting on how long she took to wash her hands. One reported that she'd scrubbed so intensely, she just had to be obsessive compulsive, and mental health pundits weighed in on the severity of her problem. The next rag reported that she simply splashed a little water on her hands and was out the door, and next to her picture was a graph comparing the cleanliness of hotel bedspreads, toilet seats, and movie theater floors to Aubergine's hands. It was all too much to live up to, but strangely enough she could control that. The hysterics of the fans, the fickle media, the frenemies in the revolving door of the nightclub circuit. It was a sort of disorder she could detach from on anything but a superficial level, and that to Aubergine defined comfort.

Still, when she was in that world, from the highs to the lows, she at a constant rate missed her siblings painfully. Tim, her North Star, lived just far enough away to be a game of phone tag, but close enough she felt he understood her. Bluebell, her U.N., picked up the phone no matter what time of night it was, responded to every text, even when they were drunken and ugly, and they were mostly all drunken and ugly. The DUI, the topless photos of her sunbathing "privately" on the roof of her beach home, the critical slaughter of her album. All her calls to them were rare and on her terms, but she could count on Blue and Tim when she needed their own breeds of reaction.

In each of these incidents her agent would somehow bail her out, and she would decide which sibling to call first. Sometimes it was Tim, whose knee-jerk response was always to make a joke about it. It eased her tendency to take herself too seriously. For instance when Aubergine said "fuck" on the Today Show and appeared intoxicated at seven in the morning, he said, "Sissy, that's a career builder right there. You lost the 'tween market, but you are the personal hero of women with really, really low self esteem." They would laugh, he would remind her that the typical American attention span is so nonexistent that people now say that "fleas have the attention span of an American," and she would be fine as soon as some other scandal came along. Big whoop.

Bluebell usually batted clean-up, but not always. Sometimes it was easier to go into a conversation with her after having Tim diffuse Auby's paranoia. Other times it was easier to vent first to perhaps the most nurturing person ever born. Bluebell could always be counted on to say "you're better than this," and to remind her of all the backbone and courage it took to get as far as she had in the industry. Bluebell truly believed in Aubergine, perhaps too much, enough that a nagging fear of being exposed for the talentless phony she felt she was plagued her every conversation with her sister. She only felt this fear with Bluebell. Big sisters come with this kind of influence, this pressure to succeed.

Flashes of her controlled chaos shot back at her in the compact mirror. She snapped it shut tight in her palm and slipped it down into the bottom of her purse. The reflection was what it was, and she wasn't too worried about paparazzi showing up at Frank Gladney's funeral. Without a mirror she swathed on the brightest, most Parisian lipstick she could dig out of her make-up kit, a little like a buffer for a girl like her. Red lipstick and her sunglasses, and she was safe.

The Amputees

The first sign Frank got that she would be a bean thrower one day, and that he would an out-the-door walker, came when he discovered what was supposed to be dusty attic fodder. It was out, brazenly, shining on the dining room table like a mirror sitting in the sun.

"You've been playing?" Frank ran his fingers down the frets.

Lorraine had just come in from raking leaves. She was a little sweaty and her curls were glued to her forehead. "I have," she said happily. "I guess I just got the itch."

Frank sat down at the table and stared at it. The itch. He'd had the itch since they moved into the house, but he was under the impression they were ignoring the itch from here on out.

"Elbows off the table, Frank."

"I can put my elbows on the table, Lorrainey," he growled. "Do you see any food here?" He never got what the fuss was about. What does it even matter, what does it fucking matter to have elbows on the table? Which great civilization collapses every time an elbow meets a table top?

"Good habits are practiced, that's all I'm saying." She removed her gardening gloves and ran them under the faucet. "These things are filthy. I think there were some dog poopies in those leaves." When he didn't respond, she hummed to herself to fill the void.

"Maybe we should play something later. Together." She turned to meet his eager gaze, surprised by his suggestion. "It's been a long time since I really heard you sing."

She shut off the water and sauntered to him. It had been far too long since she'd held his interest. She stood with a leg on either side of his knee, ran a hand through his hair. It had gotten coarse in the time since they met. No more hair gel, sideburns shorn short. His face hadn't seen the sun in twelve years, first because he spent only his nights awake, then because he spent all his daylight staring into fluorescent lamps over the factory floor. Frank looked at his wife, a faint smile masking his beleaguered life.

"I'd like that, Frank."

He gestured so that she would sit on his lap instead. He had a look in his eye, she liked it. He didn't look 34 just then. He looked like a 21 year old in that bar from way back. A cocky son of a bitch. She felt like the slip of herself she was then, light as a feather on his big hunky frame. Frank grabbed two of Bluebell's neon pencils that were sitting near her book bag. He positioned them in his hands, keeping her in his big embrace, and tapped a tune she knew she recognized on the dining table.

She crunched her forehead. "I know I know it." He looked up at her, urging her to place the song. "Can you give me more?"

Frank brought his right foot into it, working the kick drum in her mind, building a bass line for her. Finally it came to her. "Mama, she done told me, Papa done told me, too…" first softly, picking up her diaphragm as the song grew. "Son that gal you're foolin' with, she ain't no good for you…" till finally she was belting out the chorus, "Well, that's alright, mama, that's alright for you, that's alright, mama, just anyway you do-o-o," top of her lungs, working out muscles she'd forgotten about, her neck veins pulsing with life once again, "That's alright now, mama, anyway you do…" clapping softly, backing Frank up, who was backing her up.

He was refreshed.

"Elvis Presley, who? That guy can't sing. *You* can sing." Frank couldn't get enough of her when she was this way, her throat exposed to the world so that he could see her tonsils, her eyes free and confident, no agendas, no structure, just that moment right there. She never sang anymore, not that way, not even in the car with the windows rolled up. He wanted her naked.

"We should do that more often," she said.

He kissed her arm.

"I used to be a musician once, you know. Before you met me."

"You're still a musician, Lorrainey." He ran his hand down her back, tracing every notch in her spine. He smelled her skin.

"Do you miss it? Do you miss music?" Lorraine asked her husband.

He rested his forehead on her arm, ran his right hand down the inside of her thigh. "You're all I need, baby."

She ran her finger along his lower lip, his own little rock and roll sneer. "Can I make a confession?"

"Anything," he said, a little drunk off the possibility of shutting his eyes and being untethered again, naked in her apartment, a guitar on the table, all limbs and bones and muscles and measures of what of them was hard and what of them was soft.

"Sometimes," she swallowed, unaware of his moment, "I feel like you amputated me."

He stopped the rubbing, dropped his hand from her back.

"I can't explain it. I just have to fight it sometimes, you know?" He knew. "The resentment."

She had to fight resentment? He had been around the globe in search of something good and raw, and the whole time yearned like a cat in heat for her. Frank came home from Vietnam with his ugly experiences in his back pocket, but never once gave her too much of the truth, knowing her attitude on the war, knowing it would be too much monster for her fluffy little world. He then gave up his one true joy of music for a few lesser ones, the house and the security of a nine-to-five, and did it all with his shoulders back.

He never forgot the milk.

He never sulked when Bluebell had a bad dream and called for him.

He never dragged his feet when Lorraine woke him at two in the morning for a meteor shower.

He never pouted when Roscoe invited him to jam, but opted out in order to be up early for work the next day.

He did it all, and he did it all with resentment, but he did it all. And never once did he sit her down and ask for an apology.

"You don't have anything to say to me?" she asked.

He gently pushed her off his knee so he could gather himself.

"Nothing?" she pled.

"Lorraine, I was just incredibly turned on. And you tell me I've cut your legs off?"

"So sorry for the blue balls, dear," she snapped back, "but this has really been eating at me."

Frank shook his head. "Please. Get it off your chest. I really want to hear this." Best to let her talk herself right into her own grave.

She breathed in deep. "Before you, I had Lorraine Saves the Dave. I know we sucked, but it was my band. Mine. Don't you see? That night wasn't the first time we were booed off a stage. But I still loved it, every night, every practice. I loved sitting at my window to write. I used to pray for thunderstorms because that was always the time when the gods were speaking through me and the music just came."

Sometimes he loved the fruitcake in her, sometimes he absolutely fucking despised it.

"Now when I hear thunderstorms, I just get sad. I feel like that's been taken from me. I had it all, but you put a baby in me, and then stole my life from me. You gave me Bluebell, and I gave you my music."

"I was a musician before you, too, Lorraine. Did you ever think of that?" His eyes felt like they were going to combust. "I had an identity before you, too, you know."

"Frank, don't take this so personally. I'm just expressing myself."

But what she didn't realize was there was no turning back from that moment. As a couple they had a choice to live honestly and open the door to all the hate that came with it, let a new demon in every day. Or they could have kept that door closed and lived in fake harmony for the rest of their lives. Lorraine made the choice for them.

"Jesus Christ, Lorraine. Why couldn't you have just kept your goddamn mouth shut?"

Now she wasn't resentful. She was pissed off. "Don't you," shouting now, "*ever* talk to me like that!"

"All I wanted to do was take you up to the bedroom and be with you and forget all of this shit. Don't you understand? We could have erased all this if you had just kept your fucking mouth shut." Erased it for a little while anyway. "But instead, you trot this guitar out and tell me I stole it from you. Well fuck you, Lorraine. Fuck. You."

"It's not about this, you imbecile!" Lorraine bit back, snatching the guitar from the dining room table, walking it over to the back door like a wayward child. He saw her open the door but lost view of her from where he was sitting. Frank waited, he knew it was coming.

THRAWNGUH! The guitar moaned in pain as she smashed the entire thing to pieces on the back step, repeatedly. He could hear bits of wood skid this way and that on the concrete slab back there, and a final crack when she tossed the corpse out into the grass.

Lorraine walked back in, winded, and sat down at the opposite end of the table from her husband. "In the movies this is when the couple fucks each other blind."

"This isn't the movies, Lorraine," Frank looked down at his shoes, made sure they were on so he could leave. "I won't be home for dinner," he said under his breath. He grabbed his keys and left.

In the car Frank stared up at the house. On the one hand he hated this woman, he didn't understand her, wondered what level of crazy he was dealing with. On the other hand he could crawl right inside her and look out her eyes and know exactly what it felt like to be her. He realized at that moment despite all the efforts to the contrary, they had ruined each other.

An afternoon of information spilling out of them like burst fire hydrants, and only one question remained. Could he forget it ever happened and live the life he was given? Or would he spend the rest of his life asking why, lamenting the loss, aching for a dead dream?

Frank turned over the engine and made his way to the bar. The best way to forget was to remember, the bottom of his glass told him, and would tell him again and again, until only a slurry version of him lived at home.

These amputees, wheeling around each others' lives, alone in their heads, experiencing it all together but sharing none of it. Lorraine grew harder, willful in this staring contest. Frank refused to play, except for the occasional hazy screw after a night at the bar. Once he was generally delightful, lit from within by the colors and sounds of his home life. Now only the physical Frank was at home, depleting daily.

He made connections anywhere but in his own family, and his secret little life was born. The mystery of which people in his life knew him and which people in his life *really* knew him took shape.

Hard Rain

"Jesus Christ, there were fewer people along the tracks at FDR's last train ride." Tim couldn't believe the turnout. "Who are all these motherfuckers?"

Bluebell was immune by now to Tim's unique communication style. "I guess he was a little more popular than we expected." Even she couldn't believe the number and variety of people showing up, all of them dressed solemnly by their own definition, their darkest ripped jeans, plenty of black cowboy hats, and a sea of drab mu-mus.

The family walked in slow motion, like a wall of gunslingers making their way to a duel. Mark all the way to the left, in a charcoal suit and car salesman hair, appropriately austere, because Mark is nothing if not appropriate. Next to him were the Ws, all lined up and polished, shuffling along to keep up with the big kids. Then came Bluebell, looking exactly as Jackie Kennedy as she could manage, who was grateful to have found a coordinating blush veil at the last second. Then came Aubergine, who clutched her siblings' hands as tightly as she could, and worried it was wrong of her to feel sexy in her sweet black suit dress. Tim held up the other end, sunglasses on, cigarette in his mouth, staid as always, being the silent bookend he intended to be that day. "This is battle, and your only job today is to survive," Mark charged the group.

Up the steps into the church and the only available seats were up front. "Who are all these people?" Wilson asked, maybe a little too loud. A man with an unkempt salt and pepper beard and Ray Bans sat in the back row and smiled at the kid.

"Hey, little man."

Wilson's eyes surveyed the pews for any familiar faces. In front of Ray Bans there was a woman of about 400lbs. cooling her face with a large oriental fan, despite it being forty degrees outside. Nearby among the mourners was a Catholic priest with a large face tattoo. His date was a woman wearing a bleached blonde wig and a white pantsuit. A very pregnant teenager wearing a Black Sabbath t-shirt. Many, many handlebar mustaches. A woman who may have either been a very shapely policewoman, or more likely a stripper in a policewoman's costume. Two midgets, one with a seeing eye dog. Gerard Leeney. A Buddhist monk.

"I'm the most boring person here," Tim stood in awe.

"Is that the mayor?" Bluebell asked Mark. He nodded, amazed. Wilson grinned proudly.

The brood took their seats up front. Mother was there alone, perfectly resolute. She was a woman who, no matter how many shit streams flowed her way, would always persevere. "You showed!" she greeted them cheerfully, sarcastically. Bluebell embraced her and yet another tear made its way down her cheek. Mother patted her on the butt, "You've pushed out triplets, you can sit through this." That Mother equated childbirth with death should have disturbed her, but Bluebell was used to this skewed survival mechanism. It had worked for Lorraine for all these years.

The pastor opened the day with a few obligatory words. Tim wondered if he'd gotten up this morning and Googled a template for what one would say at a funeral, maybe read *Sermons for Dummies*, asked if it was this guy's first day on the job. Everything was so impersonal, sterile. He was the equivalent of a palm reader in Tim's mind. Say what the crowd wants to hear, pick up the cues, and bullshit your way to the big tip at the end. Tim wasn't judging. This was *his* plan to get through the day after all.

"I understand there were some of you who wanted to say a few words," the pastor concluded.

Bluebell edged from her seat, reluctantly, which surprised even her. She thought this would be a proud duty, but instead a flicker of her sister's prayer for a surprise tornado flashed through her brain. In the same instant she had that visual she apologized to the Lord. Bluebell's deepest honesty and faith didn't always make nice.

But wait, a temporary reprieve from another mourner, who apparently didn't understand the protocol of these things, and didn't hesitate to take to the podium to address the church. She was a beauty, Tim couldn't stop staring at her collarbones.

The stranger adjusted the microphone to her satisfaction, removed a folded up piece of lined paper from her pocket and read from it without looking up. "Hello," she said, a bit too close to the mic. Her blonde hair was silky and wavy. Aubergine stared at it enviously. "I know a few of you are wondering who I am. All of you probably." A collective head nod.

"I only knew Frank a short time. I'm a bartender at Mo's," a gentleman clapped lightly, an ill-timed endorsement. "Frank treated me good. I know I'm not the only one." Tim would have been more comfortable with a gorilla throwing its feces from the podium. But a pretty girl with kind things to say about his tormentor? His palms were wet. "I only know about Frank what I know from the bar. He came in every Tuesday for half-off PBRs. To be honest he didn't say much to me most of the time. I can think of a lot of nights he didn't say a word to me my whole shift. I guess he just liked being alone sometimes." That was some positive spin.

"Anyway, my divorce was expensive. I had no savings. I was having a hard time paying for my medication. It's not a big deal, I just get these sinus infections?" Her sentences tended to trail up into imaginary question marks. "But if I couldn't afford my meds, it made it really hard to get through my shift at work. And if I can't work, I can't pay for my meds. So it's a catch either way. I'm totally screwed, right?" This was when she started to cry. "When Frank died I was finally told that the envelopes of cash in my locker at work came from him. He didn't ask for anything in return, didn't even want me to know it was him that whole time. I mean it wasn't a lot of money to most people, but to me it saved my life." She looked down and shut her eyes to steady her emotions. "I just wanted the world to know what kind of man Frank was, even to strangers," she concluded, putting her gum back in her mouth and exiting stage right.

"Especially to strangers," Aubergine said under her breath.

And from there it was a laundry list of benevolent acts. The old folks' home administrator who came up front to thank Frank for planting those flowers last summer when a drunk driver pummeled through the previous garden. The illegal immigrant Frank taught English and US History to, advancing Javier's efforts to become a naturalized citizen.

"You gotta be kidding me," Tim complained. The siblings' ears burned with fury, even Bluebell's.

The Post Traumatic Stress psychiatrist who couldn't say much legally, but did express that Frank died a sensitive and enlightened soul, despite a tour in Vietnam that left him missing three toes. "Father had seven toes?" Bluebell asked Mother. All he ever mentioned was being "out of the country" in his younger years, but war was never brought up in her childhood home, not on Veteran's Day, or Memorial Day, or during their yearly tradition of watching *Patton* down at the Rosebud Cinema together.

The bald gentleman in the Hawaiian shirt who once played bass guitar with Frank in high school, "before groupies existed," and who credited his old friend with saving him from a disabling heroin addiction.

The little old lady who lived next door to Frank and Lorraine the past few years, who brought coffee to him every morning and every day for the past ten years, and who loved his insights on bird watching, pheasant hunting, and the perfect chili recipe. He was her daily confidante, and her days felt empty now.

On and on, down the list of grateful neighbors, band mates, bystanders, even small children thankful for the two hundred dollars he spent on candy bars every soccer season. Bluebell couldn't believe this. She realized by comparison she was near the bottom of his list of recipients of his love. Just above her siblings and her mother, Bluebell got whatever affection run-off the mailman (yearly Christmas checks) and the Humane Society (two Sundays volunteering per month for six years running) didn't need. Furious, she leaned into Mark and whispered, "What's that quote about pity?" through gritted teeth.

Mark squeezed his forehead with his fingers to find the quote among the many, then said grimly, "Let them learn first to show pity at home."

"Fucking-A right," Tim opined.

Unbelievable. Who was this man? One by one, each Gladney sibling asked themselves if they'd imagined the abuse, the neglect. Even Bluebell wondered if his showing up an hour late to pick her up after school was an exaggeration in her memory. On the scale of things, she was mistreated and had no idea until this point. Mother was smug. This was the man she knew and hung onto with bloody fingernails all those years, first by a passionate and inventive sex life, then by weighing him down with kids he didn't want. He wasn't a dream boat all those years, but she knew him before the kids did, and she knew underneath the shell was his humanity. She fell in love with it after all.

Finally, distressingly, it was the Gladney kids' turn to speak. The pastor waved them up, but none of them moved a muscle. This wasn't an unyielding resolve to protest the adulation they were witnessing, this was basic consternation. Bluebell, who previously had quite the speech typed on an index card that fit perfectly in her little navy pocketbook, even she sat there bug-eyed, trying to get her legs to move. But the brain wouldn't connect with the feet. The church sat suspended, assuming their grief was paralyzing.

Mother couldn't take it anymore. She rose, smoothed her jacket and ran a hand down either side of her hair, and progressed to the podium. Disgust, reverence, gratitude, all these emotions stirred by seeing their mother, this woman so prideful and icy, climbing the steps with her chin in the air.

"First, I want to thank you all for your words. I know I speak for the whole family when I say we were nervous about what would be said today. Frank was a," glancing toward the kids, "complicated man. You all know him for his generosity and his kindness. For that I am very proud to have been his wife all these years."

"Barf," Aubergine said. No contempt, she actually felt sorry for her mother in this one isolated minute.

"To be honest, Frank was much more withholding of his love for the people closest to him. I can't explain why. I'm not the man in the box. I can speculate, and I can run down a list of his life's accomplishments that contributed to his inconsistency. But what good does that do for any of us? Without his remorse, reasons are pointless. And let's face it, remorse is never received well anyway."

She appeared to be babbling nervously. The kids had never seen this side of her. They liked it. Bluebell said aloud, "I think she's defending us."

"Like any family, I could list some inside jokes, reasons why he was so significant a man, and why, despite the years of him rotting away in the ground out there, he won't be forgotten. But you've already done that for me, and let's be honest. We're all forgettable. So let's not consider this a history lesson. History keeps the past alive, and in the opinion of this family, Frank needs to rest already."

A very uncomfortable stillness befell the church. The pastor didn't know how to interpret Mother's farewell. A cough could be heard in the back. A baby belted out a scream and wept into her mommy's bosom. Even a baby could sense the tension and hated every second of it.

"Now I'd like to bring my children up here. They were very resistant to speak, understandably, so I'd like to send Frank off the only way this family knows how. Kids?"

Tim, Bluebell, and Aubergine looked at each other for encouragement, perhaps to agree to run out of there without having to speak. But for once, just this once in their lives, they decided to trust Mother. Slowly they rose from the pew and stood to Lorraine's rear. Aubergine's ankles shook. She'd once performed at halftime of the Super Bowl, and didn't so much as feel a butterfly. Here she trembled like a Model T.

They all stood wondering Mother's next move. All in place, she turned back to the audience and began to sing.

"Oh, where have you been, my blue-eyed son?

Oh, where have you been, my darling young one?..."

Father's favorite song. He never said so, but one could surmise it based on the number of times he'd been heard singing it while drunk. She got through the first verse alone.

"...I've stumbled on the side of twelve misty mountains,
I've walked and I've crawled on six crooked highways,
I've stepped in the middle of seven sad forests,
I've been out in front of a dozen dead oceans..."

She still had it. Lorraine's voice, without a microphone, without back-up, shot like a laser through the church, bouncing off the stained glass, choking up the pastor. Several mourners looked down at their arms for chills. Her voice was a cross between molasses and peppermint, to this day, after all this time.

"...I've been ten thousand miles in the mouth of a
graveyard,
And it's a hard, and it's a hard, it's a hard, and it's a hard..."

It had been so long since Mother's voice had been
anything but shrill. Bluebell hung her head and cried so that
the tears fell straight from her eyes to the ground, like rain.

"...And it's a hard rain's a-gonna fall..."

Tim wavered, but nothing felt more right at that
moment but to help his mother out. He came in on the
second verse, harmonizing on the bass line.

"...I saw a black branch with blood that kept drippin',
I saw a room full of men with their hammers a-bleedin',
I saw a white ladder all covered with water,
I saw ten thousand talkers whose tongues were all
broken..."

Bluebell knew he had it in him. When he was just a
kid, before she was off to college and still perfectly woven
into the family, perhaps the thread that bound them all
together for a few short years, she would hum while he
sang Pink Floyd songs. For some reason *Dark Side of the
Moon* was his saving grace even as a small child, his only
outlet. She remembered his musical ear even at that small
size, without any formal training or being prompted to try.
It was a family trait. Like big noses or freckles. If any of
these babies had come out of Mother without an innate
rhythm and sense for melody, Father would have denied
them. Frank knew his spawn when he saw it.

"...And what did you hear, my blue-eyed son?
And what did you hear, my darling young one?
I heard the sound of a thunder, it roared out a warnin',
Heard the roar of a wave that could drown the whole world,

Heard one hundred drummers whose hands were a-
blazin'..."

Tim filled to the brim with everything he could
possibly feel in one moment, his breath tightening in his
chest, suddenly sweating profusely. All those years sitting
right on the edge of sanity, all those late nights, the bottoms
of those pints, the "roar of the wave that could drown the
whole world," this was every night of his life when he felt
everything so much he went to bed drained, empty, nothing
left in him to feel, and arose the next day for a few brief
hours of indifference, before the cycle began again.

"...And it's a hard, and it's a hard, it's a hard, it's a hard,
And it's a hard rain's a-gonna fall..."

Blue and Auby knew this was their cue. They came
in on the third verse and balanced the sound, however
overwhelmed they were with pain and love and torment
and a certain liberation with singing at the tops of their
lungs in front of all of these people, their father's best
friends.

"...I met one man who was wounded in love,
I met another man who was wounded with hatred,
And it's a hard, it's a hard, it's a hard, it's a hard,
It's a hard rain's a-gonna fall...."

A fuck you and a thank you all at once. The church
could have been empty for all they cared. For ten years the
Gladneys had detached themselves from one another, ran as
far away as they could from their dysfunction, all the way
to Hollywood, to Oregon, to the highest horse of the
Lutheran faith. They indulged in everything they could-
virtue, fame, weed, booze, solitude, perfection- some days
as a distraction, others as a reminder. They lived by the
words "never look back" and thought it gave them strength,

not realizing that's all they'd done the whole time: Look back. Here they stood together at the feet of God and begged for relief, to purge themselves completely of the regret, the contempt they held, of their loneliness.

Bluebell's remorseful tears.

Mother's voice a show of defiance.

Tim expelling this succubus that he faced in his most pitch black moments.

Aubergine's voice like a beacon for other lost souls.

The Gladneys smiled at each other. Finally.

"...Where black is the color, where none is the number,
And I'll tell it and think it and speak it and breathe it,
And reflect it from the mountain so all souls can see it,
Then I'll stand on the ocean until I start sinkin',
But I'll know my song well before I start singin',
And it's a hard, it's a hard, it's a hard, it's a hard,
It's a hard rain's a-gonna fall..."

There was a certain release in this moment. No amount of healing could erase the disdain for their father or their mother, especially not in such a room drowning in Frank's good karma. Indeed there is no such thing as resolution, but there is a line drawn in the sand, a momentous decision one day. The Gladneys could never go back to the ugliness that hung over them, the near literal funk of a rotting corpse. They'd aired their dirty laundry, it was done, there was nothing left to discuss, and all without a direct word.

The song ended and the room finally exhaled. The Ws in the front row cheered, perhaps improperly, but no one bothered to stop them. Mark winked at his wife in sincere delight, and Wendy yelled, "Bravo!" repeatedly, until finally Lorraine responded with a curtsy. The rest of the church gaped at this sideshow, but then how else could Frank Gladney go out but with an improvised Bob Dylan number? It could only be outdone with a fire eater, who was likely sitting in the pews somewhere.

Finally, a thunderclap outside, and a collective spinal shiver. "Frank approves," Lorraine spoke into the microphone, and the church smiled one big smile.

Macaroni Salad

Bluebell answered the door, again. She bemoaned how unexpected the throng was for Frank's funeral and apologized for being so unprepared. Six tubs of macaroni salad went in the first twenty minutes, and now sat empty in the sink soaking. Mark did what he could to keep up with the appearance of tidiness until he eventually gave up and sat down with a glass of wine. Bluebell was embarrassed and wasn't sure how to communicate to her guests, "We just assumed everyone thought he was an asshole."

Outside it was sleeting, so inside the bizarre cross section stood and sat elbow to elbow, groin against groin. People who a few minutes earlier had never met suddenly could identify each other's after-shave. Women who normally valued their personal space were boob upon boob connecting and reconnecting with the broad spectrum of individuals who once knew Frank, and valued him enough to sit in this sweat pit and reminisce.

Bluebell couldn't bear it. "I think I just spotted a carnie in line for the bathroom."

Tim laughed, "Who are these people? When did he have time to meet them?" He was smiling. Energetic. Tim was never energetic. Intense, yes, but never energetic.

"I'm a touch claustrophobic. I feel like at any moment there's going to be a stampede."

"There will be no stampede, Blue. Just take a deep breath and relax." He held his sister's shoulders and looked at her with easy eyes. "I'll put on some music."

Tim squeezed through the crowd but couldn't get to the CD player. A roadblock of people couldn't step aside even if they wanted to, so he had to submit. He signaled to Aubergine who sat with Gerard in an intense conversation, nose to nose. They were drinking Pinot Grigio out of Wendy's teacups. All the glasses had long been claimed, and like everyone else in the house, they were making do. "Aubs!" Tim hollered over the voices. She looked up and waved. "Music!"

She caught his drift and reached over to the Play button, just barely skimming it with her fingertip while invading a neighboring conversation with her upper half. "Sorry," she said politely, and they were patient with her. John Coltrane came on and the room seemed to cool down.

Tim stood a second and watched his sister. The room could care less that they were sitting next to a falling star. No one stared, no autographs, no photographs. For the first time in ages she could sit without the dim fear of recognition. She laughed, and Gerard held her attention with a story about who knows what, her eyes animated and engaged. In his mind, Tim called this his best day.

"Timothy," the voice of his mother. He turned to see her blood red fingernails waving him toward her. He thought better than to ruin this ideal moment with whatever she had to say to bring him down. He thought about grabbing his keys and getting in the Festiva before this day could be tarnished by her derision. He reached in the pocket of his black Dickies and jingled them in his hand. She waited, reading his mind.

She could only hurt him if he let her, so he gave in and journeyed over. "Mother," he said with a sigh. She sat in the dining room along with one million other people, all of them strange. The chandelier lit her face like an interrogation scene.

"Timothy, I'm not going to eat you. Sit down."

"There's nowhere to sit. What do you want?"

She gave him the look she was famous for. Her eyes, with way too much winged eyeliner, had a way of seducing people. It didn't work on him though. He squatted to her side out of pity, and only pity. She was alone now, after all.

Lorraine gathered her thoughts and then began to speak. "Did I ever tell you how we named you?" He shook his head. She seemed happy to tell this story, despite the fact that she was telling it to him. "Well, first came Bluebell. Not your usual name. What can I say? I was in a floral phase, and when she was born all I could think of was an early Bluebell blossom. She was so compact and beautiful. Frank didn't fight me on it. I think he liked it.

"By the time Aubergine came along, our marriage was," sipping from her wine, "not so good. You see, he's a fiery man. He feels everything. He feels it too much."

"I'm aware," Tim said.

"So we parted temporarily. Did you know that? Just till the day before your sister was born. It was like she was waiting for us to reconcile to burst from her amniotic sac." Mother always used one word too many for Tim's taste. "We agreed that night that if the baby was a girl, I would name her. A boy, Frank would name him. The next day

Aubergine came, and naturally he thought it was fine, but she wasn't a boy. So he was only so interested.

"A couple of years later, you were on your way, cooking in my womb, and I knew. I just knew you were a boy. I have no idea how. I've always believed I'm psychic."

Tim found her verve strangely entertaining. He'd never seen her this sweet. "Or it was a 50/50 possibility."

"But I knew. Anyway, this was almost the exact reverse situation from your sister's birth. The night before you were born, Father and I fought about country western music. It was terrible, very dramatic. Unlike with your sister's gestation, I was full of mood swings, probably because you were a boy, so I'm sure the blame falls mostly on my shoulders. I can be abrasive at times."

"I've noticed, Mother."

"Anyway, you were born the very next day. I was alone in the delivery room. Bluebell was watching Aubergine in the waiting area, and Frank was in a bar. He didn't even know I was in labor. He came home to pack a suitcase and noticed all my belongings were missing, and put it together. He showed up at the hospital and was sent to my room, and do you know what he said when he walked in?"

"What?" Now Tim was interested.

"That son of a bitch walked in like he owned the place and said," doing her best Frank Gladney impression, puffing her chest, "'Well, what is it?' Can you believe that? He leaves me to push out a nine pound kicking and screaming child, *without drugs*, and walks in at the end like I've bothered *him*. Well, you know me and my dignity. I wasn't going to let him so much as look at you until he'd changed his tone.

"So I held you as close to me as possible. You were wrapped so tight in a blanket, you have to do that to keep babies warm, you know. So he couldn't tell if you were you, or another Aubergine. I didn't even want him seeing your face, nothing, until he calmed down and came at me any other way than that of a caveman."

Tim held his tongue. His mother appeared lovable.

"I told him so. I said, 'Frank,'" doing an impression of herself as a younger woman, which Tim found odd, "'you sit down and take a breath, because I'm not going to introduce my baby to a bully.' He said, 'Your baby? It's my baby, too.' Now this shocked me, because I'm not sure if you knew, but you were a surprise. Ah, hell, let's just come out and say it. We didn't want you."

"I figured as much."

"Don't go getting huffy. This was a long time ago. Our marriage was tenuous at best, your sister was two years old and *awful*, and here we were with another one. Try to use your imagination, Timothy. It's not personal.

"Now in spite of this being the worst thing in the world the day before, at the moment he saw you in my arms, he was downright begging for you. I told him you were a boy, and even though I had a perfectly nice name picked out for you, I would honor our agreement and allow him to decide. He sat down in that little vinyl chair they put in these hospital rooms, you know, the ugly mauve ones. I let him hold you. He had those great biceps back then. You remember those?"

"No, Mother, I don't remember how Frank looked the day I was born. You didn't exactly take pictures."

"That's true. We weren't very sentimental people." The crap on the walls of Mother's home would indicate otherwise. She poured another glass of wine and rested a hand on his shoulder, staring deep into his eyes. He let her. "Frank held you for so long. I don't know how long. Examining you, stroking your little nose, squeezing your toes. He said, 'I'm going to get him on trumpet right away. Do you see these lips?' It's true. What you had in lips... Well, what you had in lips he lacked in follow through."

Instead Tim learned the drums by mimicking whatever he could catch on the radio using take-out chopsticks. Frank always refused to eat with "gook sticks," much to Tim's inevitable benefit.

"Finally the nurse came in and he said we were ready to sign the birth certificate. His eyes were all lit up. I hadn't seen him that way in so long, Timothy. It was magical. So the doctor comes back with a clipboard and Frank does all the writing. Eventually it was my turn to sign, and I read what he wrote for your full name, 'Timothy Gladney.' No middle name. I said, 'Darling, are you sure this is the name you want? This will likely be your last chance at a boy.' I had my tubes tied that day after all. Didn't want to risk another mistake."

Tim for once found her wording entertaining and not abusive.

"Well he said to me, 'Lorrainey, there's one man I owe my life to, and it's Timothy.' At that moment I didn't know who Timothy was, but years and years later I learned this was a man he went to high school with. He said I met him once, but I don't remember it. It's bizarre, don't you think? He has a chance to name you after a great warrior or his father or a figure from Greek mythology. Instead Frank chooses a man he knew very briefly and whose last and middle name he couldn't remember for the life of him. But hey, a deal's a deal." She leaned back in her seat and let Tim absorb the information. "I always thought the name itself was a bore. But the idea was so sweet. Would you ever take your father to pay homage to anyone? Me neither," she said, skipping Tim's response.

He felt his voice crack as he said, "Thank you for telling me that." He had indeed always wondered.

"I wanted to name you Julius."

Tim flinched, "Dodged that bullet."

"Yes, too bad Aubergine wasn't spared the same fate." Tim hated to love this moment, this quiet moment alone in a room jam-packed full of chattering people. "He stayed because of you, Timothy."

His knees were sore. There was only so long he could squat after all those years behind the kit. Standing and walking were a strange ease for him. He straightened up and reached his hand to her. She kissed it quietly, patted it lovingly, and looked up into his eyes. The woman who characterized the first song he ever wrote in the seventh grade as "what an exorcism might sound like," and here she sat with her eyes trained on him, and neither of them needed to speak another word. He thought it was best to leave it at that, and so he did. The closest thing to a neat little bow he was going to get.

Weight

"Some days just need to be about thinking,"
Lorraine said, a frosted window and a white gossamer
world the distraction she needed. She just wanted to look at
nothing for a while.

"You don't want to talk about this?" Frank
grumbled. Their worlds had diverged in every emotional
way, and all that was left was whatever remained in their
lives that they physically shared. This house, the crap
they'd accumulated, one daughter they loved and who
loved them back, a daughter they had driven away, and a
son with one foot out the door. Aubergine left that morning,
and Frank was having trouble computing it all.

"What's to say, Frank? She's gone. Might be the
best thing for her."

He held it back for a second, but the hum of the
snow plow shook loose that one tear bubbling up in his
eyeball. "We failed, Lorrainey."

She knew. She knew they packed Aubergine's bags
for her from the day she was born. Every day Frank ignored
her, every day Lorraine was critical of whatever trend Auby
was starting or following- both were practically criminal, it
seemed. Their daughter walked out the door on her own
two feet, rapturously, like her real life waited. But they
pushed her out.

Frank's voice wobbled. "I thought we had more
time. I thought we could fix it."

Every day Aubergine was treated like an uninvited guest, Frank put off fixing it with her. Every day he barked at her or otherwise showed his contempt, he said that tomorrow would be the day he'd tell her the story of his life, secretly, so that they shared something, anything. He would tell her he was sorry he brought her into this. Tomorrow he'd offer to turn the clock back X amount of years and give her the option of being part of this mess, or poofing into nonexistence. But how do you tell someone they should never have been born? So the days passed.

He wanted her to know he was more than this, that he was a man once, a boy before that, and this wasn't really him. Somewhere inside a revenant of happiness existed. He hated that she was on the street and relieved to be free of him, that she would never know inside him was a real live being with joy and generosity, and he wasn't just a sad, accidental life. He wanted her to know that her mother wasn't just the appraiser of Aubergine's worth, that her mother once serenaded him from dark shadows, and seduced him with her voice once, and that once she was playful. He wanted her to know that she and her mother were the same person, and this was a good thing, the best thing.

But she was gone, and he could open the door and yell into the cold for her, but no one would hear, as if he could get his heart to speak again anyway.

Lorraine heard his cry and let herself go, too. So many years of burying whatever she had in her that was weak and real. She couldn't even remember who she really was now. All she had to be proud of was appearances, and she clutched it like rosary beads. It kept her safe, safe, safe, but alone.

Frank came and sat next to his wife, looked her in the face, put a hand on her knee. He watched her cry, his inside twisted up in itself. This wasn't what they'd hoped for all those years ago, and how it faded from that life to this one, it was the blink of an eye and one big long vegetative state all at once. "Can't we just sit here and be quiet?" she asked him.

He nodded.

Her tears came and wouldn't stop. She leaned forward and reached for his hand, the first contact they'd had in years. Frank urged from the inside, willing her to look him in the eye, hoping they were still capable of that. But holding his hand was as far as she could go.

The snow fell, and upstairs the muffled steps of their son's feet could be heard. They wouldn't let their mind go to him. That was a quiet battle of its own. Aubergine was the expressive one, the one who fought back. If they couldn't reach out to the one who actually engaged them from time to time, even if it was to scream at them, they knew even less how to connect with Tim. If he wasn't alone before, he was now. His escape was imminent, too, and they knew.

Soon Tim would be gone, and it would only be Frank and Lorraine left in that house. Seeing their youngest child go, knowing that would be the last they'd see of him, was a strange aspirin. It removed them from the immediate guilt of ruining their son. Maybe with him out of sight they could laugh again. They hoped. Frank could sit back and watch Lorraine smile and age and wrinkle, and love her again. She could dote, give him the world, pretend they hadn't spent the last sixteen years blundering through someone else's life.

It didn't work out that way though. Once Tim left, bits of Lorraine and Frank the Younger crept up around birthdays, summer solstice, New Years Eve. But mostly doors still slammed in that house, long after the relief of seeing their kids move on and reach for better lives. Platters were thrown, harsh words were exchanged. Still, they always had this quiet window.

Lorraine lived with her blinders, but every so often the truth would menace Frank, and she would do what she could to rescue him from himself. It was easier for her, but for him and the layers of his past, it was a weight he couldn't carry. "I don't have very many years to go," he told her in the tender times. He could feel it all crushing him, his heart was weak, and he wasn't fighting it anymore.

"You have to shake it, Frank," she would advise.

"You have to face it, Lorraine."

If only they could have met in the middle.

High Tide

Bluebell wasn't exactly a fan of disorder. This isn't a secret, one could tell just by looking at her. She was proud of her vast collection of sweater sets that all looked exactly alike to the untrained eye. Wilson could tell the difference between them, because he was a special breed, but the other kids assumed she wore the same outfit day after day.

Speaking of Wilson, the kids mostly ran around the room pretending to haunt it, "Like Grampa," Wendy said aloud many times, from guest to guest, using their legs as outposts for hide-and-seek, the trenches for a good game of army-man. Wilson, however, found more entertainment in sitting at the adults' feet and pretending not to hear their conversations. So much intrigue in that room! Though he didn't know what the words "bankruptcy" or "infidelity" meant, he understood they were something salacious gauging by the tone and drama of the voices saying them.

Bluebell spotted her son finally, after a good fifteen minutes checking upstairs bedrooms, the backyard, kitchen cupboards, a large purse belonging to a frail old lady, being sure to keep her nose up in search of cigarette smoke. Be he wasn't smoking, he was sitting on the ground near Auby and Gerard Leeney, scooting a small train around, making choo-choo noises. Blue watched as he pretended to be lost in his imagination, when in fact he was keeping an ear to the scuttlebutt. She leaned against a wall, busied herself by picking up spent paper plates from atop an armoire, but kept one eye on Wilson's technique.

Eventually he was done and bored and sought out his next target. The little spy crawled on his hands and knees, faux childishness, until he reached Bluebell's barricade of shins. "What are you doing down there, Mr. Wilson?"

He looked up at her on all fours so that all she could see were his eyes and the little swoop of his nose. His mouth disappeared underneath those cheeks.

She took a knee and put it to him straight. "I know what you're up to. And it's rude."

He played dumb. "Choo-choo."

"Don't even think it, Wilson. I'm smarter than you by a mile." That might have been true.

"I'm playing twains." Baby talk. He always resorted to baby talk when he wanted to swim in the sea of low four year old expectations.

"None of that. You're a bigger boy than that." She examined him momentarily. Bluebell decided to abuse her power just this once. "So. What did you overhear when you were sitting with your Aunt Aubergine?"

He thought better than to deny his mommy. "The man with the hair on his face," Mr. Leeney, "he's telling her how pretty she is. And she's acting like she doesn't know already."

Bluebell sighed. Was this good? Aubergine was barely born when Gerard was lusting after the modern incarnation of Madonna. Then again, what was better: a little flirtation from the mature, responsible, public servant, or a rodeo clown?

"Dismissed," she let Wilson off with a warning, and then stood to observe. Aubergine really was a beauty, especially like this. On Letterman her modesty was practiced and obvious to those who knew her. But sitting on this sofa, or rather packed in between the 400lb. fat fanner, Gerard, and the red-headed twins on the other side, she was genuine, and she looked clean.

Auby caught her sister's stare and winked back at her. "Hang on, Mr. Leeney," she still hadn't quite gotten the hang of this adult interaction with him. She held up a hand hoping her sister wouldn't flee, but of course Bluebell wouldn't. She waited patiently as Aubergine stepped on fingers and toes to meet her in a three foot patch of open carpet.

"Are you hitting on your music teacher?" Bluebell teased.

"I'm totally going to bone him," Aubergine cracked right back.

Bluebell giggled close like a school girl. "It's a little…"

"I know. It's a little perverted of me. I'd never hear the end of it from Tim."

Bluebell considered him. Alone and sipping from his teacup, he seemed fine. No desperation, no ego, just at ease observing the crowd, shutting his eyes to hear the jazz a little better. "You've done worse."

"I have. Two words: Mike Tyson." Bluebell's eyes shot right out of their sockets. "That was the worst, I promise."

"Holy shit."

"I know. I was there."

"No," Bluebell corrected her. "Look." She pointed with her chin over to Mother and Tim, who appeared to be in a civilized discussion, which to them signaled the flipping of the Earth on its axis. Soon, the locust invasion.

"He's *squatting* for her," Aubergine reported. "And he doesn't appear to want to kill himself."

"Not yet, but I'm sure it's coming."

"Jesus, what a weird day. Father has a legion of fans. Apparently he was nice. We sing Dylan to a church at maximum capacity and standing room only. And we sounded good, am I right?"

Bluebell admitted, "We were!" The girls high-fived.

"And now, on top of everything, those two appear to be getting along. There is a God. Or there isn't. I haven't decided exactly what this means. It's unsettling, that I know."

"Give her a chance, Sissy. After what she told the papers, you'd think you'd cut her some slack."

"Papers? Huh?"

"You didn't know? Where have you been?"

"Blue, I haven't read the newspaper since I was 19 and I was in it."

"Wilson," he was still sat at their feet, working recon. "Go get me yesterday's paper, will you?"

"Ay ay, sir!" he squeaked, and scurried off like a woodland creature.

"That kid freaks me out."

Before Bluebell could defend him, he reappeared with the Journal Sentinel. A cooperative little spy, he already had the page turned to the appropriate section. Bluebell held it up and let Auby look over her shoulder.

HOUSEHOLD NAME YESTERDAY, TODAY A LOCAL SPECTACLE

Her mug shot was splattered right underneath. She'd had better hair days. Aubergine exclaimed, "Why the fuck would I want to read this?"

"Calm down. Watch your language. Keep reading."

Auby read with her lips moving in a slurry sort of rush, "Aubergine Gladney…pop sensation…country music hack…Blue, this is journalism?"

"Keep reading," Bluebell fussed.

"…high school security guard…assault with grave intent…blah blah blah…mother Lorraine Gladney of Waukesha refused comment except to say, 'My daughter is the second coming of Janis Joplin. Unfortunately the corrupt machine of the recording industry suppressed her talent and the world will forever be void of her excellence. Now get the [sic] off my property.'" Aubergine was beside herself faced with this bombshell. "This is going to sound crazy, but I'm pretty sure this is a compliment."

The twosome watched as Tim fell a little more inside his mother's words. Lorraine had a knack for this. The push and pull of her. In low tide she was withholding, making him chase her right out to sea and finally give up as he stood there in the sand, looking down at his toes as the ocean sucked away. Then, just as his legs froze into popsicles, here she came in for high tide, making him feel grateful for even the tiniest bit of love. She did it to everybody.

"Unbelievable," Aubergine said aloud. The last compliment she'd gotten from her mother was when she was fifteen. Lorraine told her if she'd stop trying to prove to the world she was talented, she'd make a great trophy wife. This was the extent of Lorraine's affection, a put-down disguised by flattery.

Eventually the crowd thinned, but not by much. It was as if these people only had this one day to remember Frank, and the next day his great deeds would be erased from the books, his face cut out from photographs, his charity reversed. It was ten-thirty before anyone so much as yawned. This guy kept a stalwart following. They weren't leaving until Bluebell asked them to, and since Bluebell was Bluebell, the funeral rocked on.

Aubergine caught Tim's attention and waved him to the back door. Bluebell saw the signal from across the room and followed, and then Mark. No one noticed their departure except to gasp at the ice cold draft that suddenly swooshed into the room.

Outside it was November still, more November than the day before. Snow had only just fallen, and a dusting of fluff coated the patio furniture. "I love first snow," Aubergine remembered about herself, the first nice thing she'd said about Milwaukee since her arrival.

"Oh, damn. Just like that. No more fall," Mark lamented.

"Did anyone realize tomorrow is Thanksgiving?" Tim asked the group. Judging by their blank expressions, he guessed not. "How'd that get by us?"

"Are you sure?" Aubergine asked.

"Yeah. The stripper in the police lady's outfit asked if we needed her to drop off a turkey or anything tomorrow." Tim chuckled. "I told her 'sure.'"

"Why'd you do that?" Bluebell derided.

"I don't know. I like turkey, you like turkey. I thought you might like a free turkey. I didn't put it together until she was long gone." He lit up a cigarette and breathed in deep. "Sorry, Sissy, I haven't had one all day. My last one, I swear." Bluebell scowled.

"My flight leaves at three," Aubergine said to no one. Bunnies hopped through the yard looking for lovers, fearless of the great big humans standing just a few feet away.

"I'll take you on my way out of town," Tim offered.

"So that's it?" Bluebell complained. She slumped down onto a frosty chair, not bothering to wipe away the new snow. "We go back to our lives? You leave me to all this?" Mark tried not to take it personally. "I see you in ten more years?"

"Of course not, Sissy," Tim said through the cigarette in his mouth. "We'll be back. You know that." He meant it. He'd said that before and lied through his teeth. But this time he meant it.

"Because you can't abandon me again. I've been an only child for ten years now. I can't do that again." Mark wrapped an arm around her from behind and pulled her close to him. She dipped her face down into his forearm and shut her eyes.

Tim and Aubergine looked to each other for the right comforting word for their sister, but this wasn't their field of expertise. In fact they'd spent the better part of their lives avoiding her. The blood line between them was a diaphanous link, and they never understood why she was so attached to either of them. Tim and Aubergine leaned on each other because they saw the same things, heard the same cries from Mother's room, ducked from the same flying household objects. Bluebell was a world away, rushing her sorority on Frank's dime, when Tim and Auby were hiding together in their shared room, great big headphones plugged into a Y-connector on his stereo, escaping into Neil Young and the Grateful Dead, exiled just for being born. Why Blue wanted them in her life, these freaks of circumstance, they would never understand.

Tim attempted, "Sissy, don't you understand? We're those people in your family you don't invite places. We're too fucked up for you."

"For the last time, watch your language," she demanded.

"It's true, Sissy. We'll hold you back. That's all we've done since we got here. I'm amazed you didn't send us packing two days ago. You had every right."

Bluebell took a breath, then leaned deeper into Mark's arm, who subsequently wrapped her tighter in the other one, her human shaped coat. "You can't abandon me just because…" She didn't have the guts to finish her sentence.

Aubergine couldn't take the suspense. "Because what?"

Bluebell looked down beyond Mark's forearms into a crack in the concrete that ran out to the grass. Her eyes followed it all the way, wanting to straighten its crooked path using only her mind. It was helpless times like these she needed to fix cracks in the concrete. "Because I abandoned you." There. She said it.

It was quiet save for the Frankabration going on inside the house. The wine had run out hours before, but still the party trucked along. The siblings were trapped out there.

"You got a quote for us, Mark?" Tim asked.

Mark dipped his head back, as if opening his mind to whatever wisdom the heavens wanted to pour directly into his mouth. And then it came, "I sought my soul, but my soul I could not see. I sought my God, but my God eluded me. I sought my brother, and I found all three."

"Good one," Tim whispered into a cloud of his own breath.

Mold

There is no resolution.

Gerard believed this bold statement, maybe because he waited too long for his own, maybe because he was wise enough not to find romantic comedies realistic or anything to strive for. He'd spent plenty of years reading cereal boxes, watching drivers in neighboring cars while sitting in traffic, listened closely to song lyrics, hoping for that one revelatory piece of information he could be reborn by. But none of that guided him to some supreme destiny. Instead his Polaris was a string of clichés and idioms that stood the test of time, and therefore were in no way revelatory, and in every way common sense.

It is what it is.

Don't sweat the small stuff.

Time heals all wounds.

May the force be with you.

All the information he needed was already out there.

In his time on Earth, which was 15 more years than Aubergine, he'd learned that most people's lives were served better accepting what always was, instead of praying for resolution. He'd heard the word "closure" a million times before. But is there any such thing as closure? He decided there wasn't. There's no defined door slam, just one shutting so slowly and stealthily that no one notices it, or just forgets it's there. One day you wake up and realize it's been a couple of days since you thought about your dead dog, or last year's heartbreaker, and you look back and hear that flirty creak of the door, reminding you it's not quite shut yet, but almost. Then another day you don't even remember that door. It's shut, but that's irrelevant by now. Open or shut, who gives a shit? And life keeps moving.

This is as close to resolution one can expect, and to Gerard it was plenty.

Why couldn't the world see their state of being with some goddamn texture? It always bothered him. There was no need to be one thing or the other, to be troubled or stable, mature or immature. Funny or serious. Buttoned-up or casual. Clean or filthy. It was enough, better even, to be a layered overlap of just about everything. One characteristic should lead into an idiosyncrasy, and that leads into an attitude, which leads into a habit, and into a talent, into a mood. And it's all one person at once.

For instance Aubergine could one day run on the treadmill to excess, hopping off just in time not to pass out. A product of her mother's constant reminders about maintaining her taut little package, or an effort at controlling an otherwise uncontrollable world. Either excuse applied, depending on the day.

The next day she could have a thing about the volume on the television only being set on factors of four-zero is mute, four is mild, eight can be heard in the other room, twelve in the backyard, anything in between not allowed, like saying seven at a craps table. The fours were a product of learning sheet music at eight years old, when she found her gift, and finally found something steady and reliable.

And the next day she could be irritable with the man in front of her in the express lane with the 33 items on the conveyor belt. Her face would be white hot and ready to blow, the byproduct of being 22 and slighted for a song she was supposed to record but went to Britney instead. She'd never accepted that life wasn't fair.

The next day she could sit in her room and sing a Jane Arden song and impress herself, perfectly happy being her own singular audience.

The next day she could decide to just eat marshmallows in front of the TV under a bathrobe, because for too many years the world came down on her fast and hard, and hiding from it all kept her right sometimes.

Gerard just needed to get her to realize these were all the same people, and it was all so beautifully her. She didn't have to disguise today's Aubergine with whatever confines her peers felt most comfortable with her in.

A night months after the funeral, but not quite a year, Aubergine had done everything to settle in. She brought in her own linens. There was something about crisp white blankets that made her feel fresh and perfect. Gerard was fine with that.

She picked one night a week to experiment with a new recipe, learning what it means to poach something, how to stir a roux, how to destroy a perfectly nice kitchen. The rest of the week she left it to Gerard to orchestrate dinner, thankfully.

She cleared out the attic dormer, painted the walls teal, and set her laptop and electric piano next to the window. It was so high up, from the outside you might not even notice it was there. Your eyes would start at the lawn, admire the bright red door, remark on the second story window boxes, but that top window would catch the glare or hide in the shadow, and she could sit there anonymously, looking back at your squint, safely.

Gerard noticed her unease, he was no fool. He could sniff out a lost soul a mile away. He taught high school to a bunch of burgeoning artists, for Christ's sake. Insecurity was his specialty.

One afternoon they had plans to meet with friends, her new friends, his old friends, and he rushed in the door from school to be ready to leave on time. "Sorry! I know I'm late. I won't even shower. Just a quick costume change." He ran in almost without noticing her hair in a sloppy bun, no make-up. Sure, *he* loved her that way, he loved her any way, but he knew that was her signal. "Baby? What's going on?"

"I'm just not in the mood, I guess."

"Not in the mood? For wine?"

"No, I like wine. Wine sounds nice."

"So let's get some wine then. Come on, we have to hurry. Mike and Margie are saving us a table." He yanked at his necktie and pulled her upstairs with him. She resisted, pulled her arm away. "Come on. What's up?" Aubergine shrugged. "I know Mike can be obnoxious. Is that what's going on?" She didn't really know. "Is this period related?" He winced at his own reference.

She gave him the eyes. He'd seen a lot of the eyes in the past year with this new woman in his home. "I'm just not feeling like being on."

"On? Help me out here."

"You know. I've got to get dressed," making it all sound like such a process, "set my hair, brush my teeth, and then we get all the way down there, and talk, and laugh, and have a night." A chore.

Gerard was perplexed. Perplexity called for sarcasm. "Yeah, I hate laughing."

"Sometimes it's exhausting to be charming."

"Aubergine, who says you have to be charming? You can't just be there?"

"Come on."

"I'm serious," he said. He grabbed her by the waist and propped her up on the counter. She was heavier than she looked, so he let out a little groan. She found it cute. "Baby, I know you think it's your role in life to be the center of attention." She scoffed. "Don't resist that. Hear me out. What I mean is that when we go out, you make everybody laugh, you do this self-deprecating thing. 'This place is as dead as my career.' Our friends hang on your every word. And that's how it's always been, even when you were my student."

"You gross me out when you say things like that."

He waited for her to come back to now, then continued. "Aubergine, you aren't just an entertainer. You're more than that. It's perfectly fine to run out of stories, or just keep some to yourself. You can just be present, you know that?"

She rested her cheek on his chest and shut her eyes. What a scary concept. A persona that consisted of no persona at all. This might take some getting used to. In her previous life she was packaged and marketed as one particular thing, a specific breed, and if she ever stepped out of line, management and publicists would show up at her door letting her know her career was at risk. Indeed, when she went Bluegrass Pop, her search engine hits spiked, album sales plummeted. No one felt comfortable unless she fit in with their precomputed protocol. "I'm just very used to being squeezed into a mold."

"Gross! Who likes mold?" Gerard was cute sometimes. He stroked her hair, waiting for her to give in.

"Maybe you should tell Mike he can just sit there and be present sometimes. He's more than just dick jokes."

Gerard kissed her forehead, then said softly, "Oh, but he isn't."

And so it was that Aubergine simply was.

Harmony

Los Angeles was not made for people like Tim Gladney. The sun! The blasted sun. Everywhere he went, the relentless, punishing sun. It was like no one had heard of black drapery.

But! Tim was full of "buts" these days. The transition from Portland wasn't easy. He told all his friends he had to be down in Los Angeles, at least temporarily, to be closer to the studio. "Dude, L.A. is going to take you down with it," they told him.

"Yeah, **but** that's what I have to do if I want to get this album made."

"Dude, there are recording studios in Portland."

"Yeah, **but** the record company isn't going to pay a producer to live in Portland for a month. Not for a new artist."

"Dude, you're record is going to *sound* like L.A."

"Yeah, **but** so did the Doors."

"But" didn't sound like a positive word, but Tim was all about positive now. It was L.A. after all, and that damn sun was disorienting.

At the studio he resisted every producer's attempt to bring the Beach Boys out in him. Despite his new bubbly outlook, the Beach Boys didn't reside in Tim Gladney. And let's be clear. Bubbly for Tim was most people's gloom. Those who knew him recognized an incognito spirit behind his eyes. A slightly peppier walk. An un-black shirt. But gray-shirted Tim was no Beach Boy.

Luckily the record company signed him for his meditations on family, duty, politics, not for fluff. His sisters recognized a change in him when one of the songs selected for the new album was a love song. Sure, it was a song mourning his destruction of a perfectly good romance, but still, for them this represented his willingness to share his future with someone. And you don't share a future you don't want.

But! That was just one song. Tim's producer recommended a clear stand-out of the album as his first single, "The King is Dead." He and Aubergine had spent the better part of two weeks meshing her journals with his off-center ear for chord changes, and together they squeezed out the skeleton of what would be his meatiest song. At one point it was layered with a militaristic sort of percussion, a bass line that could be Tim's very own heart beating through the emotional swells of the chorus. But in the end, raw was best. Tim and his acoustic guitar, a dark studio, and the second take was the one released, no mixing to ruin its sincerity. Aubergine finally got her folk song.

"The King is Dead" would eventually play on every alternative rock station in the country, incessantly. But Tim avoided the radio for fear of watering down what went into creating the song. The less he heard it, the more genuinely he could feel what needed to be felt to deliver it to an audience who could relate to the sentiment. It was sacred. The song lost all merit if he didn't look a little pained to be playing it. As planned, whenever he did perform "The King is Dead," the lyrics burned like hot coals, and he was transported right through his life, up to his dad's funeral.

He took his first Rolling Stone interview at the Chateau Marmont, in a velvet chair he had once seen with Jim Morrison in a photograph. The reporter asked him to describe his music to a new listener. Tim spent the first few seconds stroking the chair, this surreal moment getting the full attention it deserved. He couldn't believe he was there. Somewhere in the article the reporter would write something to the effect of "Tim Gladney has arrived," and he was breathing the same air as so many predecessors he respected. *Unreal*, he thought.

Finally, "I guess it's folk music."

"You think so?" the writer doubted. "It's not too dark to be folk music?"

"I suppose to most people it's a bit bleak. But for a person like me, comparatively, it's folk music."

"A person like you."

"Well, yes. In my younger years I wrote a lot of dramatic songs, very little melody. It was warrior music. But this album is much bloodier. It was more important for me to tell a story adequately than to layer the song too much. In the past I'd bury the song under a bunch of bullshit. It was good for its time, but it wasn't very brave music, if you ask me."

The writer leaned forward and put his pencil to his lips to consider his next question. "When you put it that way, I can see it. Why do you think your approach changed so drastically?"

Tim took a breath and looked out the window onto the patio, where the Los Angeloids galloped like show ponies with thousand dollar purses, and horrifyingly to him, murses. "This is just the sort of person you become after having been that."

"So this 'folk album' is in response to that?" The reporter used air quotes, still indicating he wasn't totally convinced by Tim's analysis.

Tim shook his head. The word bothered him. "No. Never a response. It's just part of the evolution. There's no decision in it. You sit down with your guitar and a pencil, and what comes out at the time is the most organic thing. You play what you play. Like the way you dress." He gestured to the writer's slim-fitting "vintage" band t-shirt and powder blue corduroy trousers.

"You don't like the way I dress?" the writer joked.

"You dress fine. It's lovely," laughing, "even if it's something I would symbolically kill myself in." He caught himself being affable, then reeled it back in. You only get so much with Tim Gladney. "But seriously, did you dress this way in high school?"

"Definitely not."

"Of course not. And just because you didn't then doesn't mean that at some point you threw out all your clothes and decided you're only going to wear overpriced t-shirts and ass pants, right?" The reporter smiled, getting it.

"If you ran into an old friend who you hadn't seen in twenty years, they'd see you now and think you were a poser or something. But that's not fair, because they didn't see the evolution. They didn't see that one day you lost the button on those old acid wash jeans, so when you went to get new ones, they were just a little baggier, and you felt comfortable in them. And then you left those baggy jeans at a girl's house, and she dumped you, so you went and got even newer jeans, but these were a little darker, and you felt comfortable in *them*. Maybe the next pair had bigger pockets or some shit, I don't know. How many types of jeans are there? Basically what I'm saying is the acid wash guy was just as much 'you' in his day as baby blue cords guy is today. It's what feels right, so you wear it."

The writer nodded and jotted some notes.

Tim continued. "But," Tim and his buts, "It's a balance." He crossed one ankle onto his knee and began talking with his hands. He suddenly felt like he had something to really say.

"When I first got signed by the label I was so nervous. Every day I'd wake up and feel like that was the day the record deal would fall through. Even after I signed the contract, shitty bullshit contract though it was, I just felt like they would realize I was just another self-indulgent hack with too many feelings and send me back to obscurity, to Portland. So I felt this duty to be as cooperative and accommodating as possible. Have you ever felt that?"

The reporter nodded sincerely, not looking up from his notepad.

"Before we went into the studio, I hardly sang a thing. I just kind of whispered my songs to myself, practiced like crazy on my guitar. I didn't want there to be any doubts whatsoever when I got in front of the microphone. I even buffed my guitar the night before our first day. Can you believe that? I buffed my guitar."

"I don't think I've ever heard of anyone buffing a guitar before," the writer laughed. "That's so sad."

"It was! I admit it. I was pathetic. But it was stimulating to take it all so seriously. It was new to legitimately treat music like my job, because essentially over night it was my job. My sister was so shocked when I told her I'd quit smoking."

The writer butt in, "I hate to call you a liar. But you walked in here with keys and a pack of Marlboro Reds."

"Patience, man. I'm getting to that."

"My fault. Keep going," the writer scribbled away.

"So I said to my sister, 'I just want my voice to be really, really crisp when I get there.' It was like I didn't want to be revealed to be a fraud, and I was taking every precaution. I think that's every artist's fear."

"Absolutely," the writer jived.

"I was crazy. I got up early on recording day and I ate a really healthy breakfast. A grapefruit. Me. *A grapefruit*. It might have been the most effeminate I'd ever felt. I think the closest thing I'd ever eaten to a grapefruit in the past was a Red Bull." Tim focused on the sunburst coming through the big window and how everything around him radiated bright and yellow because of it. He continued calmer now, "I went out and bought an iron. *I ironed*. My sister thought I'd lost my mind."

"I can imagine."

"I got to the studio fifteen minutes before I needed to and sat there waiting, just cracking my knuckles like a son of a bitch. The production team came in really late, and every one of them was smoking like a fucking chimney. Here I haven't had a cigarette in two weeks and am at the height of a complete chemical withdrawal. One of the guys starts talking about something, I have no idea what, because all I can concentrate on is the cig' hanging out of his mouth, just kind of balancing there on his lip while he's talking. You know how it barely hangs in there like that, and it's bouncing up and down and my eyes were following it like a t-bone steak," Tim mimicked a pit bull sort of desperation. The writer laughed. "Like I didn't have enough to stress me the fuck out. Now I've got this tempter in front of me, and I can't say anything because I was so goddamned intimidated."

"What a dick," the reporter added.

"Yeah. So I get through day one of writing and rewriting and a little screwing around in the booth. We had a little powwow afterward where we kind of mapped out what we'd be doing the next day. I could tell something was wrong. They weren't nearly as excited about working with me as I was with them, that's for sure. Here I am a grown man who is fully capable of writing good music and communicating what I want, and I'm asking this guy what I need to work on to be better tomorrow. I had no mojo whatsoever. I felt like such a pussy, like I was totally surrendering my voice to them."

"Right. I get it."

"The guy looked me square in the eye, that fucking cig' still hanging there, and he says to me that there's something missing. I'm not the person who came in and played for them that first time. I don't sound like my demo. I'm too polished. Me. Polished. I could practically hear my mother's corpse cracking up. He asked me where that guy went, and he had every right to. So what else could I do?"

The writer leaned forward, fascinated now. "So what did you do?"

"I went right home and smoked a pack of cigarettes. And fuck, I know it's not good for me, but maybe it is? Maybe I'm putting too much into a smoke, but it gave me back my voice, literally and fucking figuratively, and the album flowed from there."

"I see. Balance."

"Yep. A little bit of yesterday is today, and a little bit of today is tomorrow. It's all aligned." Tim moved his hands through the air like two airplanes flying gradually closer together until they overlapped and zoomed straight out ahead of him. "Like a harmony."

Seams

"**What** do you think of this one?" Bluebell asked Mark. This one was brass and she could see her reflection in it. The other one was satin chrome, a little more understated.

Mark crossed his arms and focused on each one individually. "Which would your mother like better?"

Bluebell scoured the room for something with a little more of that Lorraine flair. And there it was. Rose gold accents with pave diamonds encrusting the lid, engraved for a slight up-charge. "Well, if we're doing something she'd like, we may as well put her in the Liberace of urns," she said, pointing to this gaudy number.

"Why are we even discussing it then? Let's just get that one." For Mark, it was open and shut.

"Is it in our price range?"

"Who cares? These are all insanely overpriced. But you don't monkey around with dollars and cents when you're picking out your mother's resting place."

"Now you're making dollars and *sense*," she joked.

"Blue. Choose now, pun later." He was trying so hard not to convey his impatience with her indecision. They'd been there for 45 minutes.

She held the ugly one in her hands and ran her fingers over all its embellishment. It was rough in her hands. "Will it match our décor?"

"No. So?"

Bluebell chewed the side of her mouth. She felt too much pressure.

"What?" Mark asked.

"Nothing. I'm just trying to think up another excuse not to get this one."

"Bluebell, it's just a jar. Okay? Think about this for what it is. It's just a jar. And this one," taking Liberace from her, "is hideous, but it's got some personality. Your mother was no brass. She wasn't stainless steel. She was *this*."

It wasn't right. Mark knew Lorraine as well as anyone could know a mother-in-law. He didn't always love everything about her, but despite that saw a glossed up version of Lorraine that spewed witticisms quicker than he could think of them, and to him she was irreverent, stubborn, and vivacious. Mark did his best, but that was all he knew about her. Bluebell knew that wasn't enough.

In the weeks since Mother's passing, Bluebell spent a lot of time alone. Coffee shops, wandering the mall with a coffee, sitting on the edge of Whitnall Park with a coffee, with her headlights on. In the dark she would sit and sip and watch the deer nibble and kiss and rub the trees. She hated hunting for this reason. These were her late night friends and preferred to believe they never got old and never were shot, and the babies stayed with their mommies forever and ever, like mythical gods. They went on and on and there were no seams. Just birth to adulthood to this park, where they ate picnic scraps and lived symbiotically with the raccoons.

All this time alone, all this coffee, and Bluebell came to some conclusions. In her life prior to Lorraine's rapid decline, a life of schedules and carpooling and family vacations, as long as she kept planning and Mark went along with them, it was all delightfully structured. Mark would tell her it wasn't necessary to micromanage her life, but this is how she'd always been. She knew every meal the family would eat, in order, and the calorie content, for the next two weeks.

She changed her eye shadow on a weekly basis, and there was a written list she kept to remind her what was next in the cycle. The week Lorraine died, it was lavender. This week's was olive green.

Every weekend she would post a communal honey-do list on the refrigerator. She and Mark would agree to tackle it as best they could, and the sooner this was so, the sooner they could do what they wanted. Nap. Watch SportsCenter. Sit at the piano and fiddle around. It burned her like a son of a bitch when Mark would skip options one through three and scratch number four off the list first. "Can't you just work your way down from the top?" Bluebell realized how irrational a complaint this was. But she was regimented, and when people would tell her so, she would say "thank you" and feel reenergized.

But what was it all for? Her eye shadow schedule didn't prevent the inevitable calamity. The family Christmas photo still came out with a glaring oversight: something green and large in Bluebell's teeth. Mark thought it was a hilarious idea to send them out anyway with a caption that read, "Humility is like underwear. Essential, but indecent if it shows." Bluebell wasn't having it, and that year hand written cards were sent instead, sans photo. She was crestfallen. Mark thought it was all a bit of an overreaction.

Perhaps she should let go of this linear life she'd mapped out so carefully. On the one hand her family was doing well. The Ws were smart and each one very unique and free to express his or herself. Mark's latest book got a mention in Vanity Fair, albeit a blip, but that blip paid for a boat.

On her wedding day way back when, Bluebell imagined a future as disciplined as her daily routine. First they would finish college, and then he would shop his book to publishers, and she would teach to subsidize the time it took before he was a success, and then would come his multi-book deal, and then the kids, all under the roof in their beautiful home on their tree-lined street. She would hustle the kids where they needed to go, and Mark would only age in the gray in his temples, sex twice a week, they would be happy, they would have it all, and at 30 they would be right where they were supposed to be.

Obviously now at her age she had learned this isn't at all how it happens. They graduated college, so that was checked off the list, which for her was a literal list in a small notebook she kept in her purse. But after that not only could she not find a job as a school teacher, nor could he get published. She worked third shift in a 24-hour convenience mart, and he went back to school for his PHD. She resented him. He was emasculated by the debt he owed for all her sacrifice. It was a strain.

In the end they did succeed, but there were months along the way they couldn't remember the last time they had kissed with tongue, much less had sex. And the definition of "success" became much more amorphous, flexing a little wider and more unattainable year after year. Reaching a goal wasn't enough. Suddenly everything good in her life was a stepping stone to something better, and that something better became yet another stone to the next something better. They could never just rest and reflect on the satisfaction of having met every dream they had conjured just years before.

When they could afford one child, four came, and though Wilson could amuse himself, the younger ones were three faces of evil at times, and sometimes she locked herself in the bathroom ten minutes longer than her shower, hiding. At 30 she knew more than at 22, but everything in between felt like false starts. A huge advance followed by a setback followed by despair followed by some accidental triumph followed by tragedy followed by fear, fear, fear. There was no milestone awareness that came with turning 30, just a day that blended with the day before. Enlightenment didn't magically appear under her pillow that morning, like a gift from the Zen Fairy.

Back to now, Bluebell felt the weight of the ugly urn in her hand and followed her gut. "This isn't right. Let's get out of here."

"Your mother is in a cardboard box on the dining room table. Eventually we're going to have to find a place for her."

"Mark, trust me on this one. She shouldn't be in a jar. Or an ugly urn."

Mark pulled her toward him and looked down her blouse. "You're very pretty."

"Now? I'm distressed," she responded, annoyed. "Do you have a proverb that can point me in the right direction?"

Mark shook his head. "I don't think this is one of those occasions where a sign tells you what to do." Because those occasions don't exist, Mark omitted. "You just have to try and make the right decision."

Bluebell mulled this over, pissed off that no solution was coming to her immediately, like some sort of mother-daughter instinct she was supposed to have. She bit a lip. This was disconcerting. "How about a quote with a curse word in it? Just because."

Mark's a machine, so he had one at the ready. Always at the ready. "Be yourself, don't take anyone's shit, and never let them take you alive."

"Not bad. Got anything else?"

"Really? I thought we had a winner."

Bluebell shook her head. "Wrong Gladney."

"Okay, how about, 'Wanna fly, you got to give up the shit that weighs you down.'" The salesperson pretended not to be listening, amused.

"Who said that one?"

"Toni Morrison."

"Hmm. It's very good, but again, wrong Gladney. I need one with some kick."

Mark dug deep into his arsenal for a good one. Finally, he snapped his fingers and lit up like a Christmas tree. "They fuck you up, your mum and dad."

"That's a quote?"

"Phillip Larkin."

Bluebell sighed, satisfied. "It's perfect. We need to get home and pack."

Shingles

"Memphis? Are you mental?" Tim exclaimed into the receiver. But in the end he went, of course. He loved an adventure. Also he'd stopped dodging Bluebell's calls a while ago, and when she got him on the phone, there was no denying her. If it's Memphis she wants, it's Memphis she gets, even smack-dab at the apex of his career thus far.

It might not have been the most orthodox way to say goodbye to their mother. Together they converged on Memphis like a special ops unit. Truth be told Blue had no idea why there and not off the top of the Eiffel Tower or floating down the Mississippi. She just knew an urn wasn't extraordinary enough. Lorraine would have only settled for sleeping with the gods.

The columns that greet you at Graceland entrance don't tell the story of what lays inside. So stately and awesome, one couldn't guess the conversations that occurred inside that would never be repeated, the quintessential Elvis moments that would never be recounted but live in the wallpaper along with the decades-old cigarette smoke. Tim thought it might be more interesting to be Elvis's gardener than Elvis himself. Aubergine imagined herself in Priscilla's furs and thick black eyeliner, deserving of all this majesty. Bluebell scanned the property, vast and unending, everything a man could need, but what an untidy life it was anyway.

Aubergine envied it all, Bluebell pitied it, Tim felt the comfort of home.

Gerard noticed the entrance was guarded by two stone lions on either side of the steps. "Who can growl the loudest?" he asked the Ws. All of them roared and held up imaginary claws, bared imaginary fangs. "I think you scared the statues," he teased. He had a knack for kids, always did. Bluebell joked this was why he was so drawn to Aubergine, but there might have been some wisdom to it. Perhaps he connected better to underdeveloped minds.

Everything hit home for Bluebell when they came to the Meditation Gardens. Elvis was under that earth, and he loved his mother and father enough to be buried right next to them, for all eternity. For a man whose line between fortune and misfortune blurred more every year he lived, Elvis always maintained that accord with them. Bluebell wondered quietly what was so special about them. Mark massaged her shoulders absently and looked on with her. "What kind of kid buries his parents in his backyard? What are they, goldfish?" He winked, she accepted.

"There are fishies down there?" Wendy asked, to the amusement of other tourists around.

Agreeing there was no way they could get away with dumping Mother somewhere in the mansion or on its grounds without being hauled out of the joint, the team agreed on a Plan B. Certainly there had been plenty of other psychos who had attempted it in the past, and so the mansion curators had come to be able to spot that wild eye a mile away. Security guards were no stranger to the fan who'd attempted to dump his wife's ashes in the pool, or behind a faux palm in the jungle room.

Instead the siblings decided they'd tour the property, make sure it felt right, and then drive as fast as they could, releasing Mother into the wind, out the sunroof. Didn't sound very sentimental, but it was ballsy, like Lorraine.

After the tour and an hour and a half of prying Ws sticky hands off of Elvis's valuables, a few souvenirs, a photo or ten on the lawn, all smiles, an experience not on the radar just a week prior, the family settled on the grass. Facing the house they felt like their own insulated little unit, and strangely significant. Gerard leaned into Aubergine's ear and said, "Pretty nice to be part of a family, isn't it?" And that's exactly what it felt like, to all of them.

Tim put Bluebell's big mom purse under his head and stretched out nice and long. Wilson crawled up next to him and rested his head in his uncle's armpit. Chitter chatter could be heard from the others, but mostly Wilson nestled down in this peace. Blue skies overhead, the occasional chortle from an obsessed tourist, but mostly just the world, and God, and quiet, and deep breaths.

"What's that, Uncle Tim?" Wilson asked softly so that no one else would chime in. He pointed to a garage with workmen atop it, apparently repairing the roof.

"That's where Elvis put his cars."

"Why are they climbing it? Are they playing?"

"No, I think they're re-shingling it, it's hard to tell from this distance." He lifted his sunglasses a second and squinted a little. "Yeah, they're putting in some new shingles, see?"

"Why?"

Mark noticed what was happening. "Oh, boy. You've started the 'why' game. You're on your own, Tim."

Tim didn't acknowledge Mark, just crossed one ankle over the other and came up with the best solution he could. "Okay, put up your hand, palm down." Wilson complied. "That's kind of like a shingle. It helps keep the roof intact. But you need more than one." Wilson put one hand on top of the other. "I like your instincts, but you have to kind of stagger it. You overlap the shingles like this," adjusting them just a bit, then added his own to the little hand roof they were making above them. "And then you add more and more, until it covers the whole thing. And the more you add, the better they overlap, the more integrity the roof has." He mimed the expansion of a roof from one shingle out wide, like a pyramid, bigger and bigger on its way down.

Wilson watched and drifted with Uncle Tim while the men worked. Off to the side about fifty feet a solitary acoustic guitar strummed "Almost Always True," a young fan in the grass near them, hair all greased up wearing 50's era wingtips, serenading his long-dead hero despite not even being born until after Elvis's brief stay.

Wendy was beat. The day wore down on her like a chore. Once they were beyond the regality of Elvis's more ornate rooms, she wasn't interested in anything besides a nap. Bluebell combed Wendy's ringlets with her fingers as she passed out on the picnic blanket, mouth open to catch whatever wanted to crawl in it. Blue suede bugs perhaps.

Gerard and Aubergine busied William by painting sideburns onto the sides of his face using liquid eyeliner she never left home without. "Okay, repeat after me, William. Thangyaverymuch," Gerard said, with as sexy a snarl he could manage. William repeated it back a little higher pitched, but in all a pretty decent start to a celebrity impression he could use at parties one day.

Watson and Mark sat side by side and discussed the triplets' upcoming birthday. "How old am I going to be?"

"You know, I'm not sure. Honey, how old is this one?" Mark kidded.

"Four, dear," Bluebell cooperated.

"So I guess that would make this your fifth birthday. That makes you a pretty big boy. Are you going to grow up a little for us this year? Be more helpful around the house?"

Watson nodded dutifully.

"That's great, buddy. Because you're mature enough now to take on some extra responsibility."

"Like a puppy?" Mark was thinking more along the lines of setting the table and making his bed. He didn't answer right away, just looked to Bluebell for whatever planned response she'd prepared for the first time any of her kids suggested such a thing. She was a woman who always had a plan, but this time her plan was to look to Wilson, who himself was on an elbow looking back to see what the verdict was.

"Wilson? Would that be okay with you?" She was in tune with her son enough to know she needed him on board. He was the gatekeeper for any new elements to the kids' routine, particularly elements he had a minor phobia of.

He felt the eyes on him, the pressure of being the crux. Watson put his hands together and pled down into them with his eyes shut, waiting. "Only if I can name him," Wilson declared, and then put his head back into Uncle Tim's pit, back to counting shingles.

"You're a rock star," Tim whispered to him.

Mark addressed his son. "You know what we say about maturity, Watson?" He shook his head. "Maturity begins to grow when you can sense your concern for others outweighing concern for yourself."

"Can I have a puppy or not?" Mark's perfect quote wasn't quite registering. Daddy smiled and Watson let out a gleeful bark.

William stood up and practiced his pelvic thrusts, swaying his hips around with a hairbrush microphone in his hand. He was really getting the hang of it.

The sounds of hammers and gabbing fans penetrated their little bubble, but the ease of the day glittered all around them. No melancholy, nothing left to resent. All that was left just was.

Eventually it was time. The sun hung a little lower and would soon hug the horizon. Mark felt a little nip starting to bite and suggested they wrap things up. They moved slowly, but the siblings agreed it had to be done. Time to dump Mother out the sunroof. It was no eternal flame, that was for sure.

Mark and the kids piled into the Astro Van, Gerard and the siblings in another car. Their driver's side windows met for one last huddle. "Once you see we've got an open stretch, hit the gas," Gerard directed Mark, who nodded in agreement. "About 35 or 40 should do it."

"You got it, Chief," Mark responded, and led the caravan. Being the last remaining cars at Graceland, they had no Elvis fans behind them to be offended by this plan, nor be hit with Lorraine's charred debris. Mark led the charge, gunning the engine as quickly as he could, one eye on the road, one on Gerard and the Gladney kids behind him.

Finally the two cars hit a comfortably whizzy speed and Gerard rolled down all the windows. Bluebell perched herself on the center console and stuck her upper half up through the top. Her hair whipped around like cotton candy, the first time in a very long while she had no concern or regard whatsoever for her helmet's appearance. "Okay!" she hollered down. "Hand me Mother!"

Tim had the cardboard box open, and passed the large baggy from the inside up to his big sister. The top was sealed with a twist tie one might use to secure a bag of bread, which at the time she thought was tacky and made a mental note to remark on later. "Here goes!" she yelled into the air, and Tim and Aubergine at once poked their heads out the side windows to watch their mother flutter down upon the grounds of Graceland.

With a few aggressive shakes Bluebell watched her mother fly through the air and leave a cloudy trail behind them. The wind picked up a bit of her and she flew a little off the road into the adjacent meadow. The further the car got away, the fainter the poof of Mother, until eventually they had to make a turn. Graceland disappeared, and they knew they'd never be back.

All heads back inside, Gerard rolled up all the windows and zipped the sunroof shut from his little cockpit control board. Bluebell faced forward, gave Mark a wave, hoping he could see the smile on her face from up there, satisfied she'd done right by Mother. Perhaps the most unorthodox memorial, Bluebell stepped out of herself to give Lorraine an appropriate send-off, and she glowed with pride.

Tim and Aubergine rested their chins on the backs of the seats and watched Memphis shift and fade, leaving Mother's mysteries like breadcrumbs behind them. The convoy trucked on back to Wisconsin, their business complete.

Along the way the cars passed through a small Indiana town that could have disappeared all together without creating much of a wrinkle in a history book. They stopped at a light and Gerard used the time to admire a Harley Davidson next to them, grumbling along happily. The man riding it couldn't be bothered to admire the sensible Ford sedan right back, which was just as well. Made it much easier for Gerard to stare.

Suddenly the bike backfired and Gerard felt his seatbelt tighten against his chest as he involuntarily jerked from his seat. Usually they sounded like gunfire, but maybe because his window was rolled up, this one sounded a lot like the loudest possible door slamming shut, "THWAM!" The biker didn't so much as smooth as his very thick mustache, cool as a cucumber.

Once he got a hold of himself, Gerard scanned his passengers for a similar reaction. He fully expected one of them to be laughing at him, probably Tim. But he was pleased to see not a single Gladney had even heard the backfire, or didn't care, because they were all peacefully oblivious.

Bluebell had her head up against the glass and was on dream number two, this one involving sequined choir

robes and an amphitheater sized parish. Tim was sitting
straight up with his head all the way back, a guaranteed
neck problem in store the next day. But Gerard liked the
relaxed expression on his face, so he let it be. And
Aubergine was using her brother's left arm as a pillow. A
string of drool dangled off her lower lip like a spider web
trying to find its point B.

The car was still. If there was a care at all in there
with them, it was asleep, too.

The motorcycle rumbled away like an angry lover,
and Gerard watched its lights as far as he could down the
highway. First two red snake eyes, then a couple of laser
points in the distance, until eventually they disappeared
into the other side of the world.

Stacy Riedel is happy you read her book, or at the very least the back cover and corresponding bio. An import from the West coast, she currently resides in Milwaukee, Wisconsin, where she writes novels and drinks a lot of coffee. Her interests include music, anything French, and creating her dogs' inner dialogs via cute voices and fictional stories. She is also co-founder and a regular contributor to your favorite website, www.bananawishbone.com.

This is Stacy's first published novel.